A Friend Like Phoebe

Phoebe went up to her room and started on her homework. It was hard to concentrate, though. She kept having fantasies about the TV show. And not just the show itself, but what could happen because of it. She might become famous! Maybe she could have her own kids' talk show, with singing and dancing and celebrities. Scenes played themselves out in her head – *The Kids' Show, starring Phoebe Gray! Tonight, Phoebe interviews Michael Jackson!* This was it! This was how she'd stand out! Let her sisters have their poems and their workshops and their modelling. Phoebe Gray was going to be on national television!

D0553357

Also available in Lions Tracks

Bury the Dead *Peter Carter*
If This is Love, I'll Take Spaghetti *Ellen Conford*
I am the Cheese *Robert Cormier*
The Chocolate War *Robert Cormier*
After the First Death *Robert Cormier*
Sixteen *edited by Donald R. Gallo*
Visions *edited by Donald R. Gallo*
The Owl Service *Alan Garner*
Happy Endings *Adèle Geras*
Kumquat May, I'll Always Love You *Cynthia D. Grant*
Haunted United *Dennis Hamley*
Second Star to the Right *Deborah Hautzig*
Rumble Fish *S. E. Hinton*
A Sound of Chariots *Mollie Hunter*
Sisters *Marilyn Kaye*
Moonwind *Louise Lawrence*
It's My Life *Robert Leeson*
Goodbye Tomorrow *Gloria Miklowitz*
Piggy in the Middle *Jan Needle*
Z for Zachariah *Robert O'Brien*
Through a Brief Darkness *Richard Peck*
Come a Stranger *Cynthia Voigt*
The Power of the Shade *Jacqueline Wilson*
The Pigman *Paul Zindel*

Marilyn Kaye

A Friend Like Phoebe

LIONS · TRACKS

First published in the United States by Harcourt Brace Jovanovich 1989
First published in Great Britain in Lions Tracks 1990

Lions Tracks is an imprint of
the Children's Division, part of
the Collins Publishing Group,
8 Grafton Street, London W1X 3LA

Copyright © 1989 by Marilyn Kaye

Printed and bound in Great Britain by
William Collins Sons & Co. Ltd, Glasgow

Conditions of sale
This book is sold subject to the condition
that it shall not, by way of trade or otherwise,
be lent, re-sold, hired out or otherwise circulated
without the publisher's prior consent in any form of
binding or cover other than that in which it is
published and without a similar condition
including this condition being imposed
on the subsequent purchaser.

For a friend like Fran Carpentier

Chapter 1

"I'm home!"

Phoebe pushed back the hood of her coat and paused in the kitchen for a response to her announcement. When none came, she went to the cake tin standing on the counter and lifted the cover. She exhaled in disappointment at the sight of the six remaining slices – exactly enough for the family dessert. She debated shaving a tiny bit off one slice, but decided it wasn't worth the risk. So she pulled off her mittens and contented herself with running a finger around the edge to pick up a little icing. Then she stuck her coat in the cloakroom and ran upstairs to her room.

The scene that greeted her wasn't particularly remarkable. Her own side of the room was in its usual state of disarray, with clothes and books scattered on the floor, and the flowered bedspread barely concealing the wrinkled sheets underneath. Her sister's side of the room was neat and organized, also as usual. And on the perfectly-made bed sat Daphne herself, looking typically dazed.

The only thing out of the ordinary was the large opened box on Daphne's bed.

"What's in that?" Phoebe asked.

Daphne didn't take her eyes off the box. She seemed transfixed. "It's the magazine." Her voice was hushed.

"The one with your poem in it?"

Slowly, Daphne nodded.

Phoebe tossed her books on her own bed and hurried over to Daphne's. "Let's see," she said, peering inside the box. Sure enough, there it was, with its recognizable shiny blue cover and red letters that read *Today's Kids*.

She was about to reach into the box when Daphne came out of her daze, little lines of worry appearing on her forehead. "Are your hands clean?"

Phoebe checked for any trace of remaining icing. "Perfectly." She stuck a hand into the box but Daphne stopped her.

"Let me take them out." Carefully, Daphne pulled out the stack of magazines, cradled them in her arms for a second, and then, gently, laid them on her bed.

"I haven't even looked inside yet," she confessed.

Phoebe didn't doubt it. Daphne liked to stretch good things out, taking her time, enjoying every second of anticipation. She took tiny licks from ice-cream cones and spent an eternity unwrapping gifts. Phoebe, on the other hand, gobbled her ice cream and tore open wrappings.

"Well, can *I* look?" she asked impatiently.

Daphne relented. "Just don't wrinkle the pages, okay?"

Phoebe tried to be as dainty as possible, using only her thumb and index finger to turn to the table of contents. It was on page 32. Quickly, she flipped towards the back of the magazine.

"Don't bend the pages!" Daphne pleaded.

Phoebe ignored her, examining page 32. There it

was – "Feelings", by Daphne Gray, aged twelve. She'd read the poem before, of course. Everyone in the family had. And when they'd learned that the poem would be published, they'd made Daphne recite it at supper time.

But the poem looked different in print, so Phoebe read it again. It wasn't her kind of poem, exactly. She liked poems that told stories, and Daphne's poems were all descriptions. But even so, she was proud of her sister.

"Wow, Daphne, you're a published poet."

Daphne smiled shyly and adjusted her dark-rimmed glasses. "It's only a children's magazine, Fee."

Phoebe rolled her eyes. How could anyone be so modest? If it was *her* name in the magazine, she'd have the words *Published Poet* printed on a T-shirt for all the world to see. "How many copies did they send you?"

Daphne gazed at the stack. "It looks like about ten. What am I going to do with them all?"

Phoebe counted on her fingers. "One each for me and Cassie and Lydia. And one for Mom and Dad."

"Just one? Don't you think Mom and Dad should each have their own?"

Phoebe brushed that aside. "They can share. 'Cause you'll need to send one to Aunt Judy and Uncle Danny, and one to Gramma in California, and you'll want some to give to your teachers – "

"Oh, no!" Daphne gasped. "I couldn't do that. They'll think I'm showing off."

Phoebe groaned. "Are you kidding? They'll probably want you to autograph them. Daphne, you're famous!" She hopped off the bed. "Let's cut one out and put it on the notice board."

Daphne went pale. "Cut up one of my magazines?"

"C'mon, Daf, you've got ten, and you just said you didn't know what to do with them all. And we always put anything important on the board."

She went over to the cluttered board hanging on the wall. Daphne joined her. "There's no space," she said.

"We'll make space," Phoebe declared. "Maybe we can take some of this stuff off – like this old report of yours. I mean, you get straight As all the time, so what's the big deal?"

"Okay," Daphne agreed. She removed the yellowed card. "How about this?"

Phoebe could barely make out the words on the faded ticket stubs. "Yeah, that was from the circus last year. We can get rid of those. What about this photo? It takes up a lot of space."

"Oh, no – let's keep that," Daphne said. "That's my favourite picture of us."

Phoebe had to admit she liked it, too. It had been taken at a family picnic the summer before, and it showed all four of the sisters. The younger ones were in front and the older ones behind them. And they looked just the way Phoebe always thought of them.

In the front, Daphne sat cross-legged on the grass. She seemed to be slightly startled, as if the camera had caught her unawares, and her glasses were perched on the tip of her nose. Behind her, Lydia was beaming, standing jauntily with her hands on the hips of her dungarees, the sun shining on her boyish haircut.

In contrast, the figure next to her had long blonde hair cascading perfectly to her shoulders. At thirteen, Cassie was a year younger than Lydia, but looked older because she wore makeup. In the photo, her all-white jumpsuit was immaculate, but Phoebe remembered how she'd wept over it later when she'd discovered the back was covered with grass stains.

Sitting on the ground in front of Cassie, arms wrapped round her knees, was Phoebe herself, wearing torn cutoffs and a Camp Ne-Hoc T-shirt. She was squinting, and her hair was light from the sun, the colour Cassie called "dirty blonde". Now, in early February, it was back to its usual plain light brown. But probably dirty.

"Okay, we'll keep the photo up here. But we can move these other things closer together." Deftly, Phoebe began pulling out drawing pins. As she removed one item, she paused to look at it.

It was a newspaper clipping, six months old. The black-and-white picture was fuzzy, but Phoebe's memory of it was very clear.

"Is that from the town council meeting?" Daphne asked, peering over her shoulder.

"Yeah." Phoebe read from the article. " 'Eleven-year-old Phoebe Gray created a stir at last night's town council meeting when she addressed the council in defence of a collection of children's books that have been brought under question. Making an eloquent plea for intellectual freedom, the youngest daughter of David and Lois Gray – ' "

11

She didn't get any further.

"What are you looking at?" Cassie walked in and snatched the clipping from Phoebe's hand.

"Hey, you almost tore it!" Phoebe yelped.

Cassie glanced at it. "Oh, it's just that old town council thing." She handed it back. "Honestly, Fee, are you still going on about that? That was a year ago."

"Six months," Phoebe murmured, carefully replacing the clipping on the board.

Cassie sniffed. "Well, you're still acting like it's a big deal. Everyone else has probably forgotten all about it."

"My magazine came," Daphne told her.

"What magazine?"

"The one with my poem in it."

Cassie actually had the courtesy to look impressed. "Oh, yeah? Let's see it." As she followed Daphne to her bed, she called back over her shoulder to Phoebe. "It's your turn to lay the table. And you'd better get it done before Mom gets home from work."

"I *know* it's my turn," Phoebe retorted. "*You're* the one who always has to be reminded." With as much dignity as she could muster, she left the room.

Cassie really got on her nerves sometimes, she thought as she began pulling out cutlery. Maybe that town council meeting didn't seem like much to her. But Phoebe counted it as the greatest moment in her life. It seemed like just yesterday that she had approached that microphone, scared to death, but determined to stop those stupid people who wanted to ban all the Betsy Drake books from the Cedar Park Public Library.

Phoebe didn't even like the Betsy Drake books, but she thought kids should have the right to read anything they wanted to. A bunch of other kids from Eastside Elementary had been there too, supporting her.

And they'd done it! They'd saved the books from being tossed out of the library. And everyone had made a fuss over Phoebe, treating her like a star. Not just her parents and her sisters, either – *everyone*, even the principal at school, told her how proud they were of her.

But Cassie was right. It was a long time ago.

When the phone rang, Phoebe started towards it, but the ringing stopped before she got there. She figured Cassie must have answered it. Her mother always said Cassie had a sixth sense about telephones – she knew when they were about to ring, and she knew when the calls were for her, which they usually were.

Phoebe was pulling a salad bowl out of a cupboard when she heard the scream. And it wasn't Cassie's standard "he-asked-me-for-a-date!" scream. This one was definitely at a higher pitch, and Phoebe almost dropped the salad bowl. She managed to set it down carefully before she ran out of the kitchen and upstairs.

The shrieks – which had not stopped – brought Daphne out of their room. The two younger sisters gaped at the sight of Cassie hugging herself and jumping up and down.

"I can't believe it! I can't believe it!"

"She can't believe what?" Phoebe asked Daphne.

"I don't know," Daphne replied, watching Cassie with interest.

Cassie stopped jumping and proceeded to give each of her sisters an unexpected hug. "That was Benson's! They picked me! *Me!*"

"Benson's?" Daphne asked.

"I think she means the department store," Phoebe told her. Cassie was now dancing up and down the hall. Phoebe ducked to avoid her swinging arms. "Hey, Cass! What did they pick you for?"

Cassie clasped her hands in rapture. "The Teen Board! I'm going to be on the Teen Board!"

Again, Phoebe and Daphne looked at each other in bewilderment. "Okay," Phoebe said. "We give up. What's a Teen Board?"

For once, Cassie didn't give them her "don't-you-know-anything?" look. She was more than happy to explain the function of the Teen Board.

"Every year Benson's picks girls to represent their juniors' department. They model in fashion shows for the store, and get their pictures in advertisements, and maybe even get to be on a TV commercial! They get a total makeover, and free cosmetics, and a discount on clothes. And I'm going to be one of them!"

"Oh, yeah?" Phoebe was impressed. "Do you make a lot of money?"

Now she did get Cassie's look. "Dummy, you don't get *paid*. It's an honour."

"Oh." Now Phoebe wasn't so impressed. It sounded like a lot of work for nothing.

"Hundreds of girls apply," Cassie continued. "Maybe thousands. And they only pick twenty. Oh, wow – I wonder if Barbie got picked, too. I'd better call her."

She didn't have to. The phone rang, and Cassie grabbed it.

"Barbie! Did you – me, too!"

Between shrieks, Phoebe heard a door slam downstairs. A second later a voice called out, "Girls! Can someone give me a hand?"

"I'll go down," Phoebe told Daphne. "Go and get your magazine." She hurried downstairs and back into the kitchen.

"Hi, Mom."

Mrs Gray set a bag of groceries on the table, ran fingers through her lightly streaked hair, and offered her daughter a hasty smile. "Start unpacking these, will you, Fee? Look at the time! I stopped at the supermarket on the way home from school and I got stuck in a queue."

Phoebe poked her head into the bag. "I hope you've got something really good in here. So we can have a celebration."

"What are we celebrating?" Mrs Gray asked, pulling off her coat.

On cue, Daphne walked in, holding up her magazine. "It's here," she said simply.

Mrs Gray took the magazine out of her hands. She opened it, found the poem, and then threw her arms around Daphne. "Sweetie, I'm so proud of you! Wait till your father sees this!"

Enveloped in her mother's arms, Daphne's face wasn't visible, but Phoebe knew it was pink. Daphne wasn't used to much attention. Phoebe was glad to see her getting the spotlight for a change.

But she didn't have it for long. Cassie tore into the room, bubbling with her news.

"Why, Cassie, that sounds exciting," Mrs Gray said. "Of course, we'll have to discuss this with your father."

"But you'll make him say yes?"

"We'll talk about it later," Mrs Gray promised. "Right now, let's talk about supper."

"We have to have something fantastic," Phoebe stated. "For Daphne."

"*And* me," Cassie added. "This is a big deal too, you know."

"Whatever fantastic dinner we come up with is for you, too," Mrs Gray assured her. "But what's it going to be?" The question was directed more to herself than the others, and the three girls watched expectantly as their mother explored the contents of the bag. She emerged with a parcel of meat and a box of pasta. "Aha! What about spaghetti and meatballs?"

The suggestion was rewarded with a general bobbing of heads.

"Now, for dessert . . ."

"We've still got the leftover cake from yesterday," Phoebe piped up.

"Mmmm . . . but we need something special," Mrs Gray murmured. "I know! Fee, call your father at work and tell him to pick up a cheesecake on the way home."

"Mom!" Cassie wailed. "I can't eat cheesecake! I'm going to be a model. I have to watch my diet."

"Watch it tomorrow," her mother advised.

Daphne smiled contentedly. "I love cheesecake."

"Me too," Phoebe said. But as she headed for the phone, she cast a regretful glance at the cake tin. She could have eaten that slice after all.

They were just sitting down to dinner when Lydia burst through the door. "Am I late?" she asked breathlessly.

Mr Gray glanced at the clock, and then gave Lydia a look of exaggerated astonishment. "Oddly enough, no. And lucky for you, too. Cast your eyes upon this feast your overworked mother has prepared."

Lydia's eyes widened as she took in the table. "Spaghetti and meatballs! And garlic bread! Fantastic!"

"If you eat that garlic bread, no one will kiss you for a month," Cassie warned her.

"I'll take my chances," Lydia said cheerfully. She gave her hands a quick wash at the sink and sat down.

"And there's cheesecake for dessert," Phoebe told her. "We're having a celebration."

"Oh, yeah? What's the occasion?"

"Daphne's magazine came. With her poem in it."

"Oh, wow!" Lydia exclaimed. "I can't wait to see it!"

"And Cassie's been chosen for Benson's Teen Board," Mrs Gray added.

"What's a Teen Board?" Lydia asked.

As Phoebe suspected, Lydia wasn't terribly impressed by the explanation. "It sounds to me like the store's using you to be a walking advertisement."

Cassie glared at her. "I *knew* you'd say something like that."

"*Girls*," Mrs Gray said automatically.

Mr Gray stroked his chin. "I don't know, Cassie. Lydia's got a point. I mean, this isn't a paying job, is it?"

Cassie's lower lip started to tremble, and Phoebe almost felt sorry for her. "You said you get a discount at the store, right?" When Cassie nodded, Phoebe turned to her father. "Isn't that sort of like getting paid?"

Mr Gray grinned. "I suppose, given the amount of clothes Cassie would buy, the money saved might be considered a rather high salary."

"Just think, Dad," Cassie implored. "I could be discovered and become a world-famous model! Wouldn't you like to see me on the cover of *Vogue*?"

"I'd rather see you pull your grades up. Is this going to interfere with your schoolwork?"

Cassie shook her head solemnly. "I swear it won't."

Mr Gray sighed. "All right."

Cassie jumped up and ran to her father. "Thank you, Daddy, thank you, thank you," she gushed as she hugged him. Then she pulled back. "Ick, you smell of garlic."

18

"So much for gratitude," Mrs Gray noted, laughing. "Oh, Lydia, there's a letter that came for you today on the counter."

As Lydia got up, Phoebe had an idea. "Why don't we cut Daphne's poem out of the magazine and have it framed?"

"That's a nice idea," her mother said. But Daphne turned to Phoebe in dismay. "Cut up *another* magazine?"

Phoebe wasn't listening. She was staring at Lydia, who was reading her letter. Her oldest sister looked stunned. "What's the matter?" Phoebe asked.

"Listen to this," Lydia said, her voice a little shaky. " 'Dear Ms Gray: You have been recommended to participate in the Illinois Journalism Workshop, a two-week programme designed for junior and senior high school students who demonstrate exemplary talent in the field of communications. The workshop will be held at the University of Illinois during the first two weeks of June.' "

She paused, and looked at her father. "What do you think of that?"

Mr Gray was beaming. "Fantastic, pumpkin. That's quite an honour."

During the chorus of congratulations that followed, Phoebe's eyes darted back and forth between her father and Lydia. Her oldest sister was always doing impressive things: marching in demonstrations, writing protest letters, starting her own school newspaper. And now she'd be going away to a university for two weeks.

She knew her father must be particularly excited.

19

As editor of the *Cedar Park Journal*, he'd be thrilled to have a daughter follow in his footsteps.

"I'm very proud of you," he was saying to Lydia. He looked round the table. "I'm proud of all you girls."

"So many accomplishments," Mrs Gray said, shaking her head in amazement. "David, have we been pushing our kids too hard?"

Mr Gray considered this. "No, I think our girls have pushed all on their own."

"Fee's the pushy one," Daphne said suddenly. "I still get shivers when I think of her standing up to the town council."

She thinks I feel left out, Phoebe thought. Did she? She wasn't sure. Both her parents had turned towards her with big smiles on their faces, and it made her uncomfortable. She had a feeling they were watching her to see if she was jealous. It was as if they were saying, We don't care that you haven't done anything wonderful lately, we love you anyway.

She tried to think of something to offer. "I got 100% in my spelling test today."

"Wonderful!" her mother exclaimed, and her father nodded with an enthusiasm that Phoebe felt was a little too much, considering that it was only an ordinary weekly spelling test.

"Now we've got a championship speller, too!" he declared. "Lois, what did we do to deserve such exceptional kids?"

Phoebe didn't feel exceptional. A perfect score on a weekly spelling test wasn't all that good. It wasn't like being a published poet, or a journalist, or even a model. Not that she wanted to be any of those.

But she wouldn't mind sharing in a little of this glory. Not one bit.

Chapter 2

Phoebe woke up the next morning feeling disgruntled. She imagined everyone in Cedar Park talking about the fabulous Gray sisters. And they wouldn't be talking about her.

She was trying not to be jealous. And she *wasn't*, not really. At least, she didn't particularly want to be doing what her sisters were doing. Even if she wanted to, she couldn't. After all, she wasn't beautiful like Cassie, she wasn't a poet like Daphne, and she didn't have her own newspaper like Lydia.

But she didn't want to be left out, either. And if her sisters were going to be great, she had to be great, too. The question was, how?

She lay very still and tried to think. All she needed was to find an opportunity for greatness. It shouldn't be *that* hard. Only her mind, still foggy with sleep, refused to produce one.

Maybe she could save someone's life. She was a good swimmer, and she could rescue someone drowning – even a man, if he wasn't too big. Too bad it was winter and the community centre pool was closed. She supposed she could push a child out of the way of a speeding car. But the roads were icy, and people were driving pretty slowly these days. They were bound to see the child and brake before Phoebe had a chance to be a heroine.

Daphne came into the room, wrapped in a dressing gown, fresh from her shower. "Fee, Mom says if you want a ride to school you'd better get up *now*."

"Okay, okay," Phoebe mumbled, but she didn't move. The only drawback to being a school hall monitor on Monday, Tuesday, and Wednesday was having to get there twenty minutes early. On the other hand, the benefit was getting a ride from her mother, who had to be at her high school teaching job around the same time.

Of course, it didn't take her anywhere near as long as her sisters to get ready for school. She didn't spend ages picking out clothes or fussing with her hair. And she didn't really see the need to take a shower *every* day. After all, it was winter, and she didn't sweat all that much.

Even Daphne, who never used to care much about the way she looked, was eyeing herself critically in the mirror.

"Maybe I should let my hair grow," she murmured.

"Why?" Phoebe asked.

"I don't know," Daphne said. "In all the pictures I've seen of poets, they have long hair. Even the men."

"Oh." It didn't make much sense to Phoebe, but she figured Daphne knew what she was talking about. She dragged herself out of bed and went out to the bathroom. When she returned, she pulled on her jeans and a heavy wool sweater. As an afterthought, she gave her hair a couple of quick brushes.

In the kitchen, her mother handed her a glass of

23

juice and went on with the conversation she was having with Lydia.

"How many kids will be at this workshop?"

"The letter said fifty kids, from all over Illinois," Lydia replied. "We'll be staying in a dorm on the campus. There'll be classes with editors from newspapers and magazines."

"Can I have some Snappy Crackles?" Phoebe interrupted. Her mother handed her the cereal box and went on talking with Lydia.

Pouring the cereal in a bowl, Phoebe looked at the box. It always had a picture of some famous person eating the cereal on it. This one had a gymnast who didn't look much older than Phoebe.

She added milk, and half-listened as Lydia rattled on about the workshop. When she paused for a breath, Phoebe broke in. "When is this workshop thing?"

"In June."

"Great," Phoebe commented. "Does that mean you're going to be going on and on about it for the next four months?"

She regretted the words the second they left her mouth. She sounded *horrid*. Lydia didn't seem to have heard her, though. She was telling their mother about her plans for the next issue of her school paper, the *Alternative*. But Mrs Gray was looking at Phoebe strangely.

"Fee, get your coat – it's time to go."

In the car, her mother glanced at her curiously a couple of times. Phoebe knew what the looks meant. Her mother wanted to talk about something serious.

Sure enough, they'd barely left the drive when her mother started. "Fee, how do you feel about all these wonderful things happening to your sisters?"

"Fine," Phoebe said promptly. She knew that wasn't what her mother wanted to hear. Whenever her mother asked her how she felt about something, she really meant, What are your true feelings? Her mother was very big on feelings.

"Because you know," her mother continued, "that we don't expect you girls to do spectacular things all the time. We love you all equally, no matter what you do."

"I know that," Phoebe said.

Her mother sighed. "When I was your age, my parents expected a lot from me, maybe because I was their only child. And I always felt I had to earn their love, by getting the best grades, or winning an award. I don't want you girls to feel that way."

"We don't," Phoebe said.

Her mother stopped at a red light and looked at her quizzically. Phoebe could tell that her short answers weren't making her mother very happy. She decided she'd better reassure her.

"I'm not afraid you and Dad are going to stop loving me," she said. "But I wouldn't mind doing something special too."

"Fee, you're special just the way you are," Mrs Gray said firmly. "You know that, don't you?"

"Sure," Phoebe said as they pulled up in front of her school. "See you later, Mom."

"I'm glad we had this talk," her mother called after her.

Phoebe nodded and smiled and waved. Sometimes it was better not to let her parents know what she was really thinking. It would only worry them. She'd rather talk about it with Linn and Melanie and Jessica, her best friends.

They'd been friends since first grade, when they'd formed a secret club, the Doodlebugs, with a secret language. They didn't use it much any more – Linn thought it was babyish. Linn was always trying to act mature.

Melanie wasn't very mature. She could get pretty silly, squealing and giggling and doing stupid things, and sometimes she drove Phoebe crazy. Jessica, on the other hand, was quiet and shy, and mostly she did whatever the other three told her to.

Even though they weren't much alike, they'd stayed best friends all through elementary school. Sometimes they fought, but they always made up. And Phoebe knew they'd understand when she told them about her sisters.

She went into the building and up to the office to get her monitor's badge. Linn was already there, putting on the belt that crossed her chest with the badge that identified her as a hall monitor.

"Hi," she greeted Phoebe. "Have I got this belt twisted at the back?"

"Yeah," Phoebe said, and fixed it for her. Then she got her own from the secretary. Draping the belt across her shoulder, she told Linn she had a problem.

"What is it?" Linn asked.

"I have to do something special," she said. Before she could go on, Melanie burst into the office.

"Doodle-doo," she called out. Linn frowned. Phoebe thought it was because Mel had used the Doodlebug greeting, but Linn looked pointedly at Melanie's tousled blonde curls.

"Didn't you comb your hair this morning?"

Melanie grinned. "Sort of. But I guess the wind uncombed it. Hey, Fee, look what I've got." She rummaged through her backpack and pulled out a copy of *Today's Kids*.

"I've only seen it a zillion times," Phoebe said. "That's part of my problem, Daphne got her poem published. Cassie got picked for Benson's Teen Board – "

"Oh, wow!" squealed Linn. 'That's fantastic!"

Phoebe ignored that. "And Lydia's going to some big-deal thing at a university for kids who work on newspapers. So now I've got to come up with something special for me."

Both of them nodded. They understood how important it was for her to keep up with her sisters.

'How about the spelling bee next week?" Melanie suggested. "I'll bet you could win that."

"Probably," Phoebe admitted. "But I need something bigger."

"We'll all put our heads together and come up with something," Linn promised.

"Maybe Jessica will have an idea," Melanie added. "Let's go to class and find her before the bell."

Linn's face grew solemn. "Jessica might be late. Her mother's back in the hospital."

It seemed like Jessica's mother was ill a lot. She

was always in and out of hospitals. "Maybe they'll make her better this time," Phoebe said hopefully.

The girls separated to go to their assigned places in the halls. A few minutes later, kids started coming in, and Phoebe was preoccupied with keeping first and second graders in line. She separated two little boys who were fighting, threatening to make them stay after school for the rest of their lives.

When the first bell rang, she checked to make sure there weren't any kids hanging round the door outside, and then went to her own classroom. Jessica was there, sitting at the back with her head bent, her long, straight brown hair falling in her face. Linn and Melanie were gathered round her desk, and Phoebe joined them.

"I'm sorry your mom's ill again," Phoebe told Jessica.

Jessica looked pale, and there were big, dark circles under her eyes. "Daddy took her to the hospital last night. She looked pretty awful."

Phoebe didn't know what to say. Jessica looked so sad, she wanted to hug her, but she knew it would embarrass her. "Maybe this time she'll be cured," Phoebe offered.

Jessica just shrugged. The second bell rang, and the girls ran to their seats.

Their teacher, Ms Lacey, got up from her desk and smiled at the class. As usual, Phoebe smiled back. Ms Lacey smiled in a way that made Phoebe feel like she was smiling just for her. She was pretty sure everyone in the class felt that way. They didn't just like Ms

Lacey – they were proud of her, too. Of all the teachers at Eastside, she was the nicest and the prettiest and the best-dressed, and she hardly ever yelled. Even when she was annoyed with them, she smiled. But it was a sad smile that said "I'm disappointed in you," and it made a person feel worse than being yelled at.

"Good morning, class," she said. "I've got two announcements to make before we start on our maths. The first one has to do with collecting coats and warm clothing for the homeless. Here in Cedar Park, we don't see many homeless people. But I was in Chicago this weekend, and I saw people huddled in doorways and sleeping on grates. Can you imagine what that feels like?"

Phoebe closed her eyes and tried to imagine it. She shivered.

"We need to help these people," Ms Lacey continued. "So if you have any winter coats at home that you don't wear any more, or heavy sweaters, please bring them to school, and I'll take them to an organization in Chicago that distributes clothing to the homeless. Yes, Ivan?"

Phoebe turned and looked at the thin, fair-haired boy who had his hand up.

"Ms Lacey, I don't think it's a good idea to give things away to these people. They should work for what they get."

"Many of these people can't work for one reason or another," Ms Lacey said gently.

"That's because they're lazy," Ivan noted.

Ms Lacey's lips tightened, and her smile was

29

strained, but her voice remained steady. "Ivan, are you personally familiar with any homeless people?"

'No, but – "

"Then I suggest you reserve any opinions you have about them until you know the facts," Ms Lacey interrupted smoothly.

Phoebe turned to Melanie in the next aisle and they exchanged triumphant grins. Ivan Fisher was a major creep, and they'd disliked him intensely since third grade when he'd first appeared in their class. Right from the start, he'd done his best to make sure no one would ever like him. His mother used to give him tons of homemade biscuits in his lunch box, and he refused to share them. Whenever he saw someone doing anything wrong – whispering, or passing notes – he made sure to bring the crime to the teacher's attention. At Break, he never wanted to take part in the games.

And he hadn't changed at all over the years. He was constantly criticizing his classmates, and he acted like he was better than the rest of them. He could be downright nasty. Phoebe was always happy to hear Ms Lacey put him down. She could say "Shut up!" in the nicest way.

As Ms Lacey continued to talk about the plight of the homeless, it occurred to Phoebe that this coat collection might be a means of getting noticed. If she brought in more coats than anyone else, maybe she'd get her name in the newspaper or something.

But then she felt guilty. Here were all these poor people sleeping in the streets, and all she could think about was getting her name in the newspaper. A good person would be thinking about the homeless, not about herself. She forced herself to concentrate on what Ms Lacey was saying.

"So, ask your parents if there are any clothes they'd like to donate, and let's see if we can help these people. And now I'd like to tell you about something exciting. Eastside Elementary is going to be on television! *National* television!"

A buzz swept through the classroom and Phoebe sat up straight.

"One of the network stations is doing a documentary on elementary education in America. Eastside has been selected as a typical suburban school, and in two weeks a television crew will be here to film part of the programme."

Robby Cooper waved his hand wildly. Before Ms Lacey could even say his name, he asked the question that was on everyone's mind. "Will we be on TV?"

A couple of kids giggled. Everyone knew that Robby wanted to be a comedian. He was probably hoping to be discovered.

"I'm not sure if they'll be filming our class," Ms Lacey replied. "However, we have been asked to select a student from this sixth-grade class to be interviewed for the documentary."

There was another buzz, this time accompanied by some applause and a squeal from Melanie. Phoebe's whole body tingled. She'd just been given a personal invitation to step back into the spotlight. This was it! This was how she'd stand out! Let her sisters have their poems and their workshops and their Teen

Boards. Phoebe Gray was going to be on national television!

Fantasies raced through her mind. What would she say when they interviewed her? It had to be something great, something that would make people sit up and take notice. "What an intelligent child!" they'd say. And she'd be famous!

Through the fog of her daydreams, she heard her name.

"Phoebe!"

"Yes, Ms Lacey?"

"That's the third time I've called you, Phoebe." Ms Lacey was wearing her disappointed smile, and Phoebe quickly shook away her fantasies.

"I'm sorry, Ms Lacey. I was . . . um . . . I was just thinking about coats for the poor people." She was surprised at how quickly this little lie came to her lips. But at least now Ms Lacey's smile was warmer.

"Well, that's commendable, Phoebe. But now we have to think about maths. Would you come to the blackboard and do the first problem?"

As she walked to the front of the class. Phoebe made a mental promise to think about the poor people later, to make up for her lie. She felt a little funny about having said that. But now it was more important than ever to shine in Ms Lacey's eyes. Ms Lacey was going to pick someone to be on TV. And she absolutely had to pick Phoebe.

All morning, Phoebe thought about passing a note to Linn and Jessica and Melanie. But there was always a chance she might get caught, and she didn't want to risk getting into trouble. So she waited until lunch time, when she could gather with them in the cafeteria.

But even then she couldn't tell them what was on her mind. Too many other kids were about.

"Can you three come over after school today?" she asked. Linn and Melanie both nodded, but Jessica shook her head.

"My father's picking me up right after school to go to the hospital."

Phoebe had almost forgotten about Jessica's mother. "Do you want us to come, too? Maybe we could all go visit her."

"No," Jessica said. "She's not allowed to have any visitors except for family. She's really ill this time."

The other girls fell silent. Phoebe had never seen Jessica look this sad about her mother before. "Maybe she'll feel better tomorrow," she offered lamely.

"I don't think so," Jessica said. She stared down at her barely-touched lunch. "I'm going back to the classroom." Abruptly, she got up and took her tray.

The others looked after her in dismay. "I don't think her mother's going to get better," Linn said. "She's always in the hospital. I think she's just going to be ill for ever."

That's the way it looked to Phoebe, too. "We have to be especially nice to Jessica," she told the others. "Maybe we can think of some way to cheer her up."

"We can make it a Doodlebug campaign," Melanie suggested. "This afternoon, let's each think of a good idea for cheering up Jessica."

Linn rolled her eyes the way she always did when

33

the Doodlebug club was mentioned. But she agreed. Then, lowering her voice, she said, "We need to talk about something else, too: this TV documentary Ms Lacey told us about. I've got an idea."

Phoebe's heart sank. Did Linn want to be chosen for the interview too? She didn't want to have to compete with one of her best friends. Phoebe tried to push this worrying thought from her mind. She'd just have to wait to find out what Linn was thinking about.

That afternoon, as soon as hall duty was over, Phoebe raced up to the principal's office to drop off her belt and badge. Melanie was already there, and Linn joined them a minute later. They retrieved their coats, hats, and scarves, and set out for Phoebe's house.

They didn't speak on the way. They couldn't, since they all had their scarves wound round their faces to protect them from the biting wind. When they got to Phoebe's and unwrapped themselves, they all started talking at once.

"I hope they film the whole class," Linn said, her teeth chattering.

"Except Robby," Melanie remarked. "He'll start showing off and he'll ruin it."

"Who do you think Ms Lacey's going to choose for the interview?" Phoebe asked, trying to sound casual.

"I know Ivan's going to ask her to pick him," Linn said. "He thinks he's so clever."

"She'll never pick him," Melanie scoffed. "I'll bet

34

even Ms Lacey thinks he's a creep. Fee, can we make some hot chocolate?"

"Sure," Phoebe said, and the others followed her to the kitchen. She went to the cabinet for the instant chocolate mix. "Okay, it won't be Robby and it won't be Ivan. What about Lorie Lester? She won the school essay contest last year."

"Lorie's clever," Linn agreed. "But Ms Lacey won't pick her – she stutters. I know that's not her fault," she added hastily, "but it takes her so long to say anything. I don't think she'd want to be on TV anyway. She gets nervous when she has to talk in class."

Phoebe put water in the kettle and turned on the gas. "What about you?" She watched Linn's face apprehensively.

Linn sighed regretfully. "I'd love to be on TV. But she won't pick me. I got two Cs in my last report. Ms Lacey says if I don't pull my grades up by the end of the month, I won't even get to be a hall monitor any more. And she's not going to pick you, Melanie, because you're always giggling."

Melanie didn't look the least bit offended by that remark. She knew it was true.

"You know who's got a good chance of getting picked?" Linn asked, grinning.

In unison, Phoebe and Melanie asked, "Who?"

"You!" Linn announced, pointing to Phoebe. "Ms Lacey likes you, and you get good grades, and she's always saying how good your oral reports are."

Phoebe tried to look modest, but it was impossible to fake it in front of her friends. "Do you really think

I've got a chance? I mean, there're twenty-five kids in our class. And lots of them have good grades."

"But Ms Lacey thinks you're mature," Melanie pointed out. "Remember when she picked the field trip leader? She said she needed someone *responsible*. And she chose you."

"But what about Keith Levin?" Phoebe asked. "He acts pretty mature. She might pick him."

"That's a possibility," Linn admitted. "But I'll bet she wants a girl. Ms Lacey's a feminist. Fee, aren't you going to make the chocolate?"

Phoebe hadn't even heard the kettle whistling. Quickly she turned off the stove, spooned the chocolate mix into cups, and poured the water. "I really want to get picked for the interview," she confessed. "I've been thinking about it all day. Do you *really* think I've got a chance?"

"Absolutely," Linn stated, and Melanie bobbed her head in agreement. "The thing is," Linn continued, "you've got to do everything you can to make sure Ms Lacey picks you."

Phoebe placed the cups on the table. "Like what?"

"Just try to impress her," Linn advised. "Make sure your homework's always done. And don't talk in class without raising your hand."

"Volunteer for things no one else wants to do," Melanie suggested. "Like picking up paper from the floor."

Phoebe nodded happily. It was great having her friends on her side. Just then the back door opened and Lydia breezed in.

"Hi, kids," she mumbled through her scarf. She

went through the kitchen and out towards the cloak-room. Phoebe moved in closer to her friends.

"Don't say anything about this in front of Lydia," she whispered. "I don't want anyone to know about it until I get picked. Then I can surprise them."

The girls barely had a chance to agree before Lydia came back in. "What's new?" she asked, making some chocolate.

Melanie started giggling, but Phoebe made a face at her and she covered her mouth. "Not much," Phoebe replied.

Lydia joined them at the table. As she sat down, she pulled two tickets from the pocket of her jeans. "Look what I got. Free passes to the new film at the Cedar Cinema."

"How did you get those?" Linn asked.

"I went by there and told the manager my news-paper is going to start printing film reviews. So he's going to give me two free passes every time there's a new film."

"Great!" Phoebe exclaimed. "Will you take me?"

"I told Sam I'd take him this weekend," Lydia said. "But I promise I'll take you next time."

"Who's Sam?" Linn asked.

"Her boyfriend," Phoebe answered.

Lydia gave her a look. "He's a friend who happens to be a boy."

"Yikes!" Melanie cried out. "Look at the time! I have to get home."

Linn had to go, too. The girls wrapped themselves up again, and Phoebe walked them to the door. As they were saying goodbye, she remembered something. "We forgot to talk about Jessica. We were going to think of ways to cheer her up."

"Oh, yeah," Linn said. "We'll do that tomorrow over at my house after school, okay?"

The girls left, and Phoebe went up to her room. She wanted to get started on her homework right away and make sure it was perfect.

A copy of *Today's Kids* lay on her bed. *If I get famous*, she thought, *I'll probably get my picture on the cover of* Today's Kids. *Maybe on a grown-up magazine, too. Maybe even on a cereal box!*

And as she opened her maths book, she happily envisioned the Snappy Crackles pouring out from the top of her head.

Chapter 3

Early the next morning, just out of the shower, Phoebe stood in front of the cupboard and pondered its contents. There wasn't much to think about on her side, but she had to consider each item from a particular point of view – Ms Lacey's. What was most likely to impress her teacher?

Behind her, she heard Daphne stir. "What are you doing?"

"Picking out something to wear to school," Phoebe replied.

"Are your jeans dirty?"

Phoebe glanced at the rumpled pile of denim on the floor. "Probably," she said. Of course, that had never stopped her from wearing them before.

"Fee!" Daphne exclaimed. "That's a summer dress. You'll freeze if you wear it today."

Phoebe fingered the material. It *was* kind of skimpy. Reluctantly, she replaced it. "I don't know what to wear."

"You sound just like Cassie," Daphne commented. "Why do you want to get dressed up today, anyway?"

Phoebe turned and faced her. She was never very good at keeping secrets, but Daphne was. And she was dying to tell somebody. "I might get to be on TV in two weeks," she told her sister. And she explained the situation.

Daphne's reaction was just what she'd hoped for. Her sleepy eyes widened, she sat up in bed, and her mouth made an O. "Television! Fee, you could be famous!"

Phoebe nodded happily. "But first I have to get chosen. So I need to do everything I can to make sure Ms Lacey thinks about me."

Daphne got out of bed and joined Phoebe in front of the cupboard they shared. "What kind of clothes do you think she likes?"

Phoebe contemplated this. "Proper clothes. The kind that match. But not too stylish. She doesn't approve of sixth graders being too fashion-conscious."

Daphne pulled a tartan skirt out of her side of the cupboard. "This might be a little long on you, but you could roll it up at the waist. And I've got a pullover that goes with it." She rummaged through her drawer and got it out.

Phoebe's eyes gleamed. It was just the kind of outfit Ms Lacey would probably approve of: neat and boring.

"Your hair's a little tangled at the back," Daphne noted. "I'll brush it if you want."

Phoebe allowed her to do that. She winced when the brush tugged at her tangles, but she didn't complain. She was feeling very kindly towards her sister. It was really good that Daphne didn't display the least bit of jealousy at the idea of Phoebe's becoming famous. Her other sisters would be green.

"Listen," she said suddenly, "don't tell the others about this, okay?"

"I won't," Daphne assured her. "I guess it would be embarrassing if they all knew and then you didn't get picked."

"Oh, I think I'll get picked," Phoebe said, hoping she didn't sound too cocky. "If I do everything right. But I want it to be a surprise."

"Gee," Daphne sighed. "I wish I had your confidence."

Phoebe beamed. Already she was feeling successful.

She dressed quickly and hurried down to the kitchen. She was eager to see if the clothes made any sort of impression.

They did. Cassie's mouth fell open, Lydia's eyebrows shot up, and her mother looked positively stunned.

"Fee, you look lovely!" her mother exclaimed. "What's the occasion?"

"Nothing special," Phoebe replied airily. "I just felt like dressing up."

Cassie recovered from her shock and looked at Phoebe knowingly. "What's his name?"

"Whose name?"

"The boy you're dressing up for."

Lydia glared at her. "Did it ever occur to you that a girl just might want to dress up for herself, *not* because of a boy?"

Cassie considered this. "No."

Personally, Phoebe preferred Lydia's style to Cassie's. Lately, Lydia had been getting into colours, and today she was wearing a bright purple sweatshirt with baggy red pants. Phoebe thought the outfit

41

looked great, but it wasn't the kind of look that would impress Ms Lacey.

She thought of something else that would dazzle her teacher. "Mom, do we have any old coats or sweaters? We're collecting them at school for the homeless." She envisioned herself marching into the classroom with an armful of clothes.

"Probably," Mrs Gray said. "I'll check this afternoon."

"But don't give away any of Daphne's stuff," Phoebe added. "I might need her old clothes."

Her mother looked at her quizzically. "Where did this sudden interest in clothes come from?"

"I don't know," Phoebe said vaguely. "I just feel like looking nice. Can we go now?" She wanted to get Linn's reaction to her new look.

Her mother smiled. "My baby's growing up." Her tone was wistful, and Phoebe wished she could tell her that as soon as the TV show was over, she'd go right back to being a sloppy kid. But her mother would just have to deal with a mature Phoebe for a couple of weeks.

In the principal's office at school, Linn pronounced her outfit perfect. "Now be sure to stop at Ms Lacey's desk when you go in the room," she said, "and make sure she notices what you're wearing. And remember to volunteer for stuff and raise your hand a lot, especially during social issues. You know how she hates it when we don't talk in social issues."

Phoebe nodded in agreement as she strapped on her monitor's belt. "I hope it's civil rights again."

Melanie hurried into the office. "Has anyone talked to Jessica?"

"I tried to call her last night," Linn said. "But there was no answer. I guess they were all at the hospital."

Phoebe realized she hadn't thought of Jessica once that morning. She wasn't being much of a friend. "Let's try to cheer her up in class," she said to the others.

"I don't know," Linn said. "If her mother's as ill as she says, maybe she won't even come to school today."

But when they got to their classroom after hall duty, Jessica was there. Linn and Melanie hurried over to her. Phoebe was about to follow, but then remembered her mission. She paused at Ms Lacey's desk.

The teacher was looking at some papers on her desk. Phoebe coughed to get her attention.

"Ms Lacey, when are we having the spelling bee?" She knew perfectly well when it was scheduled, but it was the only thing she could think of to ask the teacher.

"Next Wednesday," Ms Lacey said, looking up. "My, you look very nice today, Phoebe."

Mission accomplished! "Thank you," Phoebe said politely. She hurried to join her friends at the back of the room and report on her first success of the day. Her smile faded when she saw their faces. Jessica looked even worse than she had the day before.

"What's the matter?"

Linn spoke in a whisper. "Jessica's mother's in a coma."

"What's a coma?" Phoebe asked. Whatever it was, it had to be something pretty bad.

Jessica's voice shook. "It's like being asleep, and they can't wake her up."

Phoebe didn't know what to say. She thought for a minute. "Maybe that's good for her. Maybe if she has a good, long sleep, she'll wake up and feel better."

"My mother always says sleep is the best medicine," Melanie added.

Jessica didn't seem convinced. The bell rang, and they took their seats. Phoebe kept turning to look at Jessica. She'd never seen her friend act like this before, even all the other times her mother had gone into the hospital. But she forced herself to face forward when Ms Lacey started talking.

Phoebe wasn't able to put her plans into action during maths. Ms Lacey didn't call on her, even though she raised her hand each time the teacher put a problem on the board.

Her big opportunity came during social issues. Ms Lacey loved social issues. She always said that kids should know what was going on in the world and what people were talking about. She even wanted them to argue about these things.

"Today we're going to talk about television," Ms Lacey announced. "Many people feel that some of the most popular programmes on television shouldn't be shown, or that certain programmes should only come on TV late at night, when children can't see them."

Gina Allston raised her hand. "What kind of programmes?"

"Well, for example, programmes that contain violence. We all know that there's a lot of violence on television, particularly on all those police and detective shows. How do you feel when you see people shooting each other on TV?"

Phoebe's hand shot up. This was one of her mother's pet peeves, and sometimes she complained when the girls watched action-packed TV shows. Phoebe had never thought about it much, but she knew what her mother would say. "Those police shows are too violent. People kill each other and act as if it's no big deal. It's not like real life."

Ivan Fisher was waving his hand wildly. "I agree with Phoebe," he said. Phoebe glanced at him in surprise. Ivan hardly ever agreed with anyone. "It's not good for kids to see all that killing," he continued. "I think there should be a law that TV shows can't have so much violence."

Phoebe shook her head at him. *She* hadn't said anything about a law. He was acting like they were on the same side, and she didn't like that one bit. Who wanted the support of a major dork?

Ms Lacey was also shaking her head and frowning slightly. "You're suggesting that television should be regulated by the government. That's the policy in Communist countries."

Robby Cooper didn't bother to raise his hand. "Isn't *Ivan* a Russian name?" he blurted out.

"Hey, Ivan – are you a Commie?" yelled Charles Gleason.

Ms Lacey clapped her hands together twice, her standard method of shutting them all up. "That's

45

enough! I don't want any silly name-calling. Ivan and Phoebe were both presenting important arguments, and we should respect them."

Phoebe cringed at hearing her own name linked with Ivan's. Again, she waved her hand. "Ms Lacey, *I* don't think there should be laws for what can be shown on TV."

"Neither do I," replied Ms Lacey.

Phoebe felt relieved.

"But what's the answer?" Ms Lacey continued. "On the one hand, we're confronted with TV shows we don't approve of. On the other, if we try to stop the networks from showing these programmes, we'll be imposing our tastes on other people. Yes, Gina?"

"I think we should have the freedom to choose what we watch on TV, and not have the government tell us what we can watch."

"Good point." Ms Lacey beamed at Gina.

"But if there were laws, people wouldn't watch programmes that aren't good for them," Ivan protested.

"Go back to Russia," Robby yelled, and once again Ms Lacey clapped her hands sharply.

Phoebe quickly raised her own hand. "In America, everyone has a right to an opinion." She smiled kindly at Ivan. "Even Communists."

"I'm not a Communist!" Ivan yelped in outrage.

Ms Lacey sighed. "We know you're not a Communist, Ivan. But Phoebe's made an excellent point. In a democracy, we have the freedom to express our opinions, and the freedom to choose from those opinions. Perhaps allowing violence on television is a sacrifice we must make in order to ensure our country's freedoms."

At that point, she started talking about the Constitution and the Bill of Rights, and Phoebe relaxed. She glanced at Linn, who shot her an "okay" signal.

Phoebe didn't get another chance to impress Ms Lacey until just before noon.

"I don't want to spoil your lunch," the teacher said, "but when you get back, we'll be having a little surprise quiz on your social studies assignment." When the students groaned loudly, Ms Lacey just smiled. "Sorry about that," she added, though she really didn't look the least bit sorry.

Phoebe saw a chance to stand out from the crowd, and said the first thing that came to mind. "I think surprise quizzes are good for us," she declared. "They keep us on our toes."

Half the class, including Linn, turned and stared at her in disbelief. Even Ms Lacey looked startled. "Well, thanks for your support, Fee," she said lightly.

The class lined up to go to the cafeteria. No talking was allowed in the halls, but as soon as they entered the cafeteria, Robby and Charles cornered Phoebe.

"Hey, Fee," Robby yelled, "maybe if you ask real nice, Ms Lacey will give us *two* surprise quizzes."

"Yeah!" echoed Charles. "Since when are you running for teacher's pet?"

Melanie came to her defence. "Oh, shut up!" It wasn't much, but it was better than nothing.

Unfortunately, Ivan stepped in. "I agree with Phoebe. Personally, I think surprise quizzes are an excellent idea. Those of us who read our assignments have nothing to worry about. Isn't that right, Phoebe?"

Phoebe winced. Why was he suddenly paying so much attention to her? She decided it was best just to ignore him.

Unfortunately, the other boys didn't do the same. Charles started laughing like a hyena, and Robby leered at Ivan. "Hey, man, what's going on? Are you two in love, or what?" A couple of other boys started hooting, and Phoebe could feel her face get hot. She grabbed Linn's arm. "C'mon, let's get our trays," she mumbled urgently.

They got their lunches and hurried over to their usual place. Phoebe slammed her tray down on the table. "Ivan Fisher – *ick*!"

"Remember last Christmas when the class drew names for presents?" Melanie asked. "He wouldn't do it because he said he might have to get a present for someone he didn't like."

"He's such a creep," Linn noted.

"They're all creeps," Melanie declared. "All boys, I mean."

"But Ivan's the creepiest," Phoebe said. "The rest of the boys just act stupid. Ivan's really awful."

Linn examined her sandwich. "Why are sixth-grade boys so immature?"

"I think it's nature," Phoebe sighed. "Girls mature faster than boys. What kind of sandwiches are these?"

"Mystery meat." Linn took a bite and chewed thoughtfully. "When do the boys catch us up?"

"I don't think they ever do," Melanie replied,

peering into her soup. "What do you think these things in the soup are?"

Phoebe ran a spoon through her own bowl. "Everything we had yesterday, chopped up. Boys have to catch up sometime. I mean, when we're eighty years old, will they be acting like they're seventy-five?"

"Those boys we met last summer at the pool weren't so bad," Linn remarked. "Chip and Leonard and what's-his-name. Remember the one you liked, Jess? What was his name?"

Jessica was intent on turning her jelly into liquid by flattening it with her spoon. She didn't seem to have heard Linn's question.

"Jess?"

She looked up blankly. "Huh?"

Phoebe suddenly remembered a time when her own mother had had the flu. She'd been in bed for days, and everyone had tiptoed round the house, talking in whispers. For a while, Phoebe had thought her mother would never get better. She shivered.

"Let's pool our money and send flowers to Jessica's mother in the hospital," she suggested.

The faint ghost of a smile appeared on Jessica's face, but disappeared quickly. "She won't be able to see them. She's in a coma."

"But they'll be there when she wakes up," Phoebe insisted. "We'll go to the florist after school, okay?"

Linn and Melanie nodded. Jessica continued to flatten her jelly.

"Uh-oh," Linn said suddenly. "Look who's headed this way."

Phoebe turned slightly and groaned. Ivan, who usually sat alone, was coming towards them, clutching his lunch box. He *would* be the type who still brought his lunch from home, Phoebe thought.

"May I sit down?" he inquired politely.

Phoebe didn't reply. A flat "no" would be just too rude, and besides, she was too busy wishing for a hole to appear in the floor.

Linn took over. "We've finished eating. And we're going back to class in exactly five seconds."

"I just wanted to tell Phoebe something," he said plaintively.

Phoebe raised her eyes warily. She didn't like his expression. It was too friendly. "What do you want?"

No one invited him to sit down, but he did anyway. "I just wanted to tell you that I'm not a Communist."

Melanie started giggling. Phoebe stared at him in disbelief. "Who said you were?"

"You sort of did, in class."

Phoebe sighed. "Look, Ivan, I don't care if you're a Communist or not."

"But I'm not," Ivan insisted worriedly. "If anything, I'm the opposite. I don't even believe in social welfare! I think the individual should look out for himself, don't you?"

Phoebe gazed at him blankly. "Ivan, I don't even know what you're talking about." With that, she rose and picked up her tray. Melanie and Linn followed, and after a little nudge, so did Jessica. Without saying goodbye to Ivan, they headed to the racks, where they left their trays.

50

"I guess I was pretty rude," Phoebe remarked in the hall.

"You have to be rude to boys like Ivan," Linn noted matter-of-factly. "Otherwise you'll never get rid of them."

Back in the classroom, there were a couple of other kids who had returned early to cram for the surprise quiz. It was a sixth-grade privilege to be able to leave the cafeteria whenever you wanted to. But since there wasn't anywhere to go besides the classroom or the cloakroom, it wasn't much of a privilege.

A few minutes later, everyone was back, including Ms Lacey. The teacher opened a drawer and pulled out a stack of papers. "Ready for your quiz?"

There was the usual response, more loud groaning, but Ms Lacey wasn't the least perturbed. "I'll just pretend I didn't hear that. Everyone, close your books and put them away."

She was beginning to pass out the tests when the classroom door opened. Phoebe could see the principal, Mr Hoffmann, stick his head in and beckon to Ms Lacey.

They had a brief, hushed conversation at the door, and then Ms Lacey turned to the class. "Jessica," she called out softly, "could you come out to the hall, please?"

Phoebe watched what little colour was left drain from Jessica's face. Slowly, as if she was sleepwalking, her friend rose from her chair and went out in the hall with Ms Lacey.

A few seconds later, Ms Lacey returned. Without

speaking, she gathered Jessica's coat and books, and took them out to the hall.

By now, everyone in class was murmuring. Phoebe and Linn exchanged worried looks. People didn't get called out of class for just anything. But maybe it was good news, Phoebe thought. Maybe Jessica's mother had woken up.

Finally, Ms Lacey came back. She didn't have to ask for silence or attention. Everyone's eyes were on her unusually serious face as she leaned back against the desk and gazed out at them.

"I have some very sad news to tell you. Jessica's mother died today."

Phoebe sat very still. As the teacher's words sank in, she felt a shiver that seemed to begin in the pit of her stomach.

"Jessica's mother has been ill for a very long time, but that doesn't mean this isn't a terrible shock for Jessica. There is no way a person can be prepared for a parent's death. I'm sure Jessica will not be in school for the next few days. When she returns, I hope you will all be very, very kind and understanding."

Kind and understanding. Phoebe could hear the words, but they seemed to come from very far away. She was dimly aware of a bobbing of heads throughout the room. She would have nodded too, except that the chill in her stomach had spread through her entire body. And she was frozen inside.

Chapter 4

Phoebe was feeling peculiar. Maybe it was being dressed up on a Monday night. Cautiously, taking pains not to wrinkle her skirt, she sat down on the edge of her bed and stared at nothing. Lydia appeared at her door.

"What time are we going to Jessica's?"

"As soon as Mom's ready," Phoebe replied. "She's getting dressed now. Do I look okay?" She got up from the bed and smoothed the pleats in her plain navy blue skirt.

"Fine," Lydia said. "How about me?"

"Fine," Phoebe echoed. Lydia looked terribly grown-up in her dark green skirt with its matching jacket. It wasn't Lydia's usual style, but Phoebe figured it was right for the occasion. Not that Phoebe had ever had any experience with this kind of occasion. She'd never paid a condolence call before. She wondered if everyone there would be crying.

"When did they have the funeral?" Lydia asked.

"Yesterday, in Indiana. That's where Mrs Duncan came from." She paused. "Have you ever been to a funeral?"

Lydia shook her head. "But it must be awful, watching someone get buried. Imagine seeing your mother being put into the ground."

Phoebe didn't want to imagine it. Secretly, she was

glad the funeral had taken place out of town so she didn't have to go.

"I'm going downstairs," Lydia said. "You coming?"

"In a minute."

As soon as Lydia left, Phoebe began practising. "I'm sorry your mother died," she said softly. No, that sounded awful. She tried again. "I feel terrible about your mother." That didn't sound right either. Maybe it was the "mother" part. Maybe she could just say "I'm sorry" or "I feel terrible".

She went across the hall to her parents' bedroom. Through the open door, she watched silently as her mother finished dressing. She looked really pretty in her grey dress with a single strand of pearls.

Mrs Gray looked up and saw her. "Fee, come here and zip me up, would you?"

As Phoebe approached her, she sniffed the familiar scent her mother always wore. Carefully, she slid the zipper up the back of her mother's dress. When she finished, her mother turned and kissed her on the forehead. Impulsively, Phoebe threw her arms around her and buried her face in the soft wool.

She was probably crushing her mother's dress, but Mrs Gray didn't seem to mind. Gently, she stroked Phoebe's head.

"Why did Mrs Duncan have to die?" Phoebe's voice was muffled, but her mother heard her quite clearly.

"I don't know, darling," she said simply. "There's no explanation. We just have to accept it."

Phoebe lifted her wet face and looked up at her

mother. She felt so frightened. She wanted to say something like "Mom, don't die," and hear her mother tell her she never would.

"Lois!" Her father's voice boomed from downstairs. "It's almost eight. Let's get going."

"Mom," Phoebe said urgently, "what should I say to Jessica?"

Her mother smoothed Phoebe's hair. "Just give her a big hug and tell her you love her."

The others were waiting for them in the living room. Daphne was holding a cake Mrs Gray had baked earlier, Lydia carried a casserole dish, and Cassie had some flowers their father had brought home from the florist. Phoebe was empty-handed, but maybe that was okay. She'd need both arms for hugging.

"Why do people bring food and flowers when someone dies?" she asked as they piled into the car.

"The food is so that the family won't have to think about cooking," her mother replied. "As for the flowers – well, to tell you the truth, I don't know. I suppose it's just a token, to let people know you care."

It was not far to Jessica's house. The drive was full, and cars were parked bumper-to-bumper in the front. Mr Gray had to park some way away.

"Who are all these people?" Daphne asked as they walked up to the house.

"Neighbours and friends, I assume," Mr Gray said. "Did Jessica have a big family, Fee?"

"No, I don't think so. I mean, she doesn't have

any brothers or sisters. And all her relatives are in Indiana."

A woman who was a stranger to them opened the door. She introduced herself as a neighbour and ushered them in.

Phoebe had never spent much time at Jessica's. Mrs Duncan was ill so much of the time that the girls rarely gathered there. Phoebe looked round. There were a lot of people, mostly grown-ups wearing dark clothes and talking quietly in small groups. Phoebe spotted Mrs Cavanaugh, Linn's mother, talking to Mr Duncan. Through the archway leading into the dining room, she saw a table covered with food, but no one seemed to be eating. The air smelled so sweet from all the flowers that it made her dizzy.

Mr Duncan approached them. Like Jessica, he was tall and thin and pale. His face was sad, but at least he wasn't crying. He shook hands with Mr Gray, and Mrs Gray kissed him on the cheek. Then he greeted the girls, admired the flowers, and thanked them for the food.

Mrs Gray directed Daphne and Lydia to place the cake and casserole on the table, while Cassie went with the neighbour who had opened the door to put the flowers in a vase.

"I know Jessica will be glad to see you," Mr Duncan said to Phoebe. "She's in the kitchen."

Phoebe nodded, but she didn't move.

"Go on, darling," her mother urged.

Again Phoebe nodded, and started toward the kitchen. She paused in the dining room to look at the food. Was all this food just for Jessica and her father?

she wondered. How would they ever eat all these cakes? There was a big platter of fried chicken, too – Phoebe's favourite. She wasn't hungry, but she stood and looked at it for a while.

Finally, she went out to the kitchen. Jessica wasn't alone. Linn was there, sitting on the kitchen table, chewing on a celery stalk. She started to grin when she saw Phoebe, but then seemed to remember why she was there. The grin turned into a sort of sickly smile.

Jessica looked even skinnier than usual in a black velvet dress. She was standing by the window, staring out, and drumming her fingers on the sill.

"Hi," Phoebe said awkwardly.

Jessica turned. "Hi."

Phoebe went over to her, still not sure of what she was going to say. Then it felt perfectly natural to do exactly what her mother had advised. She hugged Jessica and whispered, "I love you."

Jessica didn't return the embrace, but she didn't pull away, either. When Phoebe released her, Jessica's face was a little pink. But she just gave Phoebe an embarrassed smile and said, "Thanks."

There was a moment of silence. Now what? Phoebe wondered. "Um, how are you feeling?" It was probably a stupid question under the circumstances, but it was all she could think of.

Jessica shrugged. "Okay." Her voice was listless, and there were deep, dark circles under her eyes.

"How come you're in here?"

Jessica studied the floor. "Too many people out there. They keep looking at me."

Phoebe understood. Jessica never liked being the centre of attention.

"Isn't Jessica's dress pretty?" Linn asked. Phoebe rolled her eyes. Linn sounded like she was talking about some little kid. She hated it when Linn put on her superior "I'm-so-mature" act.

But Jessica didn't seem to mind. She always liked having Linn's approval. "It's not too long?"

Phoebe spoke quietly. "No, it's a nice dress. I've never seen you wear it before. Is it new?"

"My aunt bought it in Indiana. For the funeral."

"Oh."

Luckily, there was a distraction. Melanie came in, went straight to Jessica, and threw her arms round her. "Oh, Jess," she cried out. "I'm so sorry about your mother."

Phoebe held her breath. Melanie was the first to actually say it out loud. Would Jessica start crying now?

She let out her breath when she saw that Jessica's eyes were still dry. "Thanks," her friend said. "What's going on at school?"

"Not much," Melanie replied, hopping up on the table. "Did Fee tell you Ivan's still hanging round her?"

Jessica actually looked interested. "Oh, yeah? Do you think he's got a crush on you?"

"That's what everyone thinks," Linn said. "The boys have been teasing Fee like crazy."

"Poor Fee," Jessica said sympathetically.

Phoebe couldn't believe this conversation was taking place. Here her mother had just died, and

Jessica was acting like she was more concerned about stupid Ivan Fisher.

But as Linn went on to describe Phoebe's latest encounter with the class nerd, Phoebe noticed that Jessica looked a lot less depressed than she had a few minutes before. Maybe this was what she needed – to be distracted, to think about ordinary things so she wouldn't think about her mother.

Linn was mimicking Ivan's voice, and Jessica was giggling when the kitchen door swung open. Mr Duncan came in, followed by Mrs Gray. Everyone stopped talking immediately, but Mr Duncan looked pleased to see Jessica acting normally.

His voice was gentle as he spoke to her. "Jessica, I've been thinking. You know, your mother's parents wanted us to come back to Indiana and stay with them for a while, a few days, or maybe a week. But I don't want to keep you out of school any longer."

Mrs Gray went over to Jessica and put an arm round her shoulder. "We were wondering if you'd like to stay with us. Daphne's offered to sleep on the couch, so you could share Phoebe's room. How does that sound to you?"

Jessica looked at Phoebe nervously, and Phoebe nodded with vigour. She thought it was an excellent plan. She could keep Jessica distracted and be a real friend to her.

"Okay," Jessica said. "I suppose I'd better go and pack some stuff."

"I'll help you," her father said, and the two of them left the room.

Mrs Gray remained. "I suppose I should have

asked if this was okay with you first, Fee. But I didn't think you'd mind."

"I don't mind," Phoebe said. She liked the idea. Jessica always made her feel good, the way she looked up to her and listened to her. Now Phoebe could help Jessica feel good.

"I knew you'd agree," her mother said, giving her a quick hug. She included Melanie and Linn in her smile. "And I know all you girls want to help Jessica through this. You three are her best friends, and right now she needs your love and support."

The three girls nodded solemnly.

"I'm going to see if she needs any help," Mrs Gray said. When she left, the girls, were silent for a minute. Phoebe felt like she'd been handed a mission.

"I think we should make a Doodelbug vow," Melanie announced. For once, Linn didn't groan at the mention of the Doodlebugs. They hadn't done a Doodlebug vow in ages. The last one Phoebe could remember was the year before, when they'd pledged never to tell anyone that Melanie still slept with a teddy bear.

They formed a tight circle and took the position, crossing their arms and holding each other's hands. Since it was Melanie's idea, she started.

"We, the Doodlebugs, vow to do everything we can for Jessica."

Linn went next. "And we vow to help her not feel too sad."

Now it was Phoebe's turn. What was there left to say? She thought for a minute. Then it came to her.

"And we vow to think more about her than ourselves."

Linn looked puzzled. "What do you mean?"

Phoebe tried to explain. "I mean, like, if Jessica wants to do something, and we want to do something else, we ought to go along with what she wants to do."

"But Jessica always does what we tell her to," Linn objected.

"That's just it," Phoebe said. "I think she just goes along with us because she's too shy to say what she really wants. We should help her to stand up for herself."

Melanie didn't look convinced. "How is that going to help her feel better?"

"It will," Phoebe insisted. "Daphne said that when *she* started standing up for herself instead of always listening to Cassie and Lydia, she started feeling a lot better about herself."

Melanie and Linn shrugged. "Okay," they chorused.

Phoebe had a feeling they didn't really understand. But they'd catch on. Phoebe had plans for Jessica. She was going to show her what a real, true friend she was.

Chapter 5

Phoebe yawned loudly as her mother pulled the car up in front of Eastside Elementary. Mrs Gray looked at her through the mirror above the dashboard. "Did you girls stay up half the night talking?"

"Not me," Jessica assured her. "I was so tired I fell asleep the minute I got into bed."

"And I wasn't reading under the covers, either," Phoebe added quickly. That was the truth, too. She was sleepy because she'd lain awake in the darkness, making plans for Jessica.

Her mother pushed the lever that opened the boot of the car. "Don't forget the bags," she said as the girls got out. Phoebe and Jessica went to the back of the car and pulled out the two bags of coats and sweaters Mrs Gray had collected. Together, they slammed the boot shut and waved to Mrs Gray as she pulled away.

"I hope Ms Lacey doesn't make a big fuss," Jessica said as they lugged the bags into the school.

"About the clothes?"

"No," Jessica said. "About my mother." Her head was down, and Phoebe had to strain to hear her. "I'm afraid I'll start crying. I don't want to cry in class."

Phoebe understood completely. Crying in front of a teacher would be a totally humiliating experience. "I'll try to distract her," she promised.

"Thanks," Jessica said. "You're a real friend."

Phoebe smiled modestly.

Ms Lacey was at her desk grading papers when the girls walked in. When she saw them, she got up and headed straight for Jessica.

"Jessica, dear, I'm so glad you're back. We've missed you." Jessica kept her head low and mumbled something like "thank you".

Phoebe watched Jessica's face closely for any sign of tears.

Ms Lacey put a hand on Jessica's shoulder. "I was terribly sorry to hear about your mother. I know this is a very difficult time for you, and I want you to know that you can talk to me about it any time you want."

Jessica was blinking rapidly. Phoebe took the cue, and stepped forward. "Ms Lacey, I—"

"Just a minute, Phoebe." Ms Lacey was looking at Jessica intently. "You know, Jessica, I lost my own mother just last year, so I do understand how you must be feeling."

Now Jessica's face was scrunching up. "Ms Lacey!" Phoebe said urgently.

Ms Lacey turned to her. "What *is* it, Phoebe?" Her voice was testy.

"I brought some clothes for the homeless," Phoebe announced.

"That's nice, Phoebe, but I'm talking to Jessica right now."

"I . . . I have to go," Jessica stammered. Turning rapidly, she fled the room.

Ms Lacey looked after her with concern. When she turned back to Phoebe, her expression changed.

"That was rude, Phoebe," she said sharply. "You shouldn't interrupt like that."

"I didn't mean to be rude," Phoebe replied. "I was just afraid Jessica might start crying."

"There's nothing wrong with crying. It can often make a bereaved person feel better. Perhaps you should be showing a little more concern and sensitivity."

Phoebe's mouth fell open. She was speechless.

"I do appreciate your bringing the clothes," Ms Lacey continued. "Now I think you'd better get going if you're on hall duty."

As Phoebe backed away to the door, the teacher added, "And try to be more understanding about Jessica."

Phoebe managed to nod before she hurried out of the room. Once in the hall, she tried to sort out what had just occurred.

Ms Lacey had thought she didn't care about Jessica! How could that have happened? And here she'd stayed awake half the night trying to think of ways to make her friend feel better!

Suddenly she realized something awful. If Ms Lacey was annoyed with her, if she thought Phoebe was an uncaring person, she'd never pick her to be in the television documentary!

Phoebe ran to the principal's office, but Linn and Melanie had already picked up their belts and gone to their positions. Quickly she got her own belt, and dashed off to find Linn. It was almost time for the doors to open, and she had to hurry.

"You're not going to believe what just happened," she told Linn breathlessly. She recounted the conversation in the classroom.

"You better do something about that," Linn warned. "You don't want Ms Lacey to have bad feelings about you."

"I know!" Phoebe exclaimed. "But what can I do?"

For once, Linn wasn't ready with advice. And then the bell rang. Phoebe had to run to get into her position on time. She couldn't afford to get into any more trouble.

Even as she was ordering the first graders to shut up, she desperately tried to think of some way to get back into Ms Lacey's good graces. She had to let the teacher know she really cared about Jessica. And it wouldn't be enough just to tell her. She had to show it. But how?

When Phoebe returned to her classroom after hall duty, she still hadn't come up with any brilliant ideas. Jessica was already in her seat, and Phoebe noticed several kids stopping by her desk and going out of their way to greet her. Poor Jessica, Phoebe thought. She looked positively unnerved by all the attention. But this time Phoebe wasn't going to risk interfering.

She was momentarily distracted by the unwelcome appearance of Ivan at her desk. "Are you prepared for the spelling bee tomorrow?" he asked.

"I guess so." Phoebe didn't look at him as she

spoke. She didn't want to encourage him to continue the conversation.

"I've been practising for a week," Ivan told her.

Who cares? Phoebe thought. She wished he'd go away. Out of the corner of her eye, she could see Robby watching them and grinning. Any minute now he was bound to make a loud comment.

"I expect you and I will be the closest competitors," Ivan continued. "I'd wish you luck, but I intend on winning myself. I suppose you feel the same way."

Fortunately, the bell rang and he had to take his seat. Phoebe shuddered. Why was he being so chummy? He was acting like they were *friends!* Ivan didn't have any friends. And for as long as she'd known him, he'd made it perfectly clear he didn't want any.

The morning passed uneventfully, and Phoebe didn't have any opportunities to score points with Ms Lacey. She wasn't called on to do any of the maths problems. And they spent longer than usual on maths, so there wasn't time for social issues.

Just before lunch, someone asked Ms Lacey about the television documentary.

"I don't have any more information about it," Ms Lacey told them. "And before anyone asks, no, I haven't decided which of you will be interviewed."

Ivan put up his hand. "Will grades have anything to do with your decision?" The rest of the class exchanged knowing glances. Ivan was a straight-A student.

Ms Lacey looked thoughtful. "Of course we'd

want a good student representing us. But I think the person selected should have more than high marks. We want a student who is mature and serious, but outgoing, too. We don't want to choose a person who will see this as an opportunity to be a star." She glanced significantly at Robby Cooper, who grinned and pretended to slide under his desk.

"We're looking for someone who's sensitive to the general needs of all students," Ms Lacey continued. "Someone who cares about other people."

Great, Phoebe thought dolefully. And now she thinks I don't even care about one of my best friends.

At lunch time, she gathered with her friends, and they discussed her predicament.

"You better study for that spelling bee tomorrow," Linn warned.

"Ivan said he's been practising for a week," Phoebe said. "I haven't even looked at the word list."

"You probably don't need to," Melanie assured her. "You're a natural-born speller."

"I'll practise with you tonight," Jessica offered.

Phoebe smiled wanly. "Thanks, Jess. But it's going to take more than a spelling bee if I'm going to show Ms Lacey I'm sensitive and mature."

"Don't sweat it," Melanie advised. "No one in our class is all that mature. I still think you've got a good chance."

"Sure you have," Jessica said encouragingly. "You're all those things Ms Lacey was talking about." She sighed. "I wish I was."

"What do you mean?" Phoebe asked.

Jessica bit her lower lip. "Did you ever notice how Ms Lacey never picks me for anything?"

"That's because you never volunteer," Linn reminded her.

"I know." Jessica looked positively mournful. "I wish I wasn't so shy. My mother—" For a second, she faltered. "My mother always said I should try to be more outgoing."

The girls looked at her in surprise and Phoebe knew why. Jessica had always been shy. It was one of those things they'd taken for granted about her and hadn't thought about much. Only Phoebe had suspected that Jessica might not be happy that way.

"*Ominous.*"

"O-M-I-N-O-U-S."

"Good," Jessica said. "Now, *revelation.*"

"*Revelation,*" Phoebe repeated. "R-E-V-E-L-A-T-I-O-N."

"Excellent. *Perceive.*"

"Perceive. P-E-R-C-I-E-V-E."

"Uh-oh," Jessica said. "Remember, '*i* before *e*, except after *c.*'"

"Oh, yeah – right." Phoebe groaned and fell back on her bed. "Want me to read some words out to you now?"

"It wouldn't do any good," Jessica replied. "I don't have a chance."

"Why do you think that? You always do well in spelling tests, don't you?"

"Oh, sure," Jessica agreed. "But I'll mess it up tomorrow. I get flustered in front of people."

Phoebe sat up. "You know, Jess, you don't have to be shy if you don't want to be."

Jessica stared at her. "That's what my mother used to say."

"And she was right! Why are you so afraid of people?"

Jessica turned pink. "I don't know. I guess I'm afraid I'll say or do something stupid and people will laugh."

"So what if they do? Jerks like Robby Cooper are always laughing at other people. You either ignore them, or you laugh right back at them."

Jessica smiled slightly. "It's easy for you to say. You're so brave."

"Not all the time," Phoebe assured her. "Last summer when I had to stand up in front of the town council, I was scared stiff! But you have to force yourself to do things like that. And then you feel really good."

"Yeah?" Jessica didn't look convinced.

"Just try it," Phoebe urged. "It takes practice. Tomorrow in class, volunteer for something. And don't get nervous during the spelling bee. Just keep telling yourself you know the words. So what if people are looking at you? They can't hurt you."

Jessica seemed to be deep in thought. Phoebe wondered if her friend had even heard her. "I'm going to have a bath now," she said, leaving Jessica alone with her thoughts.

Later that evening as they were getting into their beds, Jessica asked Phoebe a question.

"Fee, do you believe in heaven?"

Phoebe didn't have to think about that. "Yes, absolutely."

"Me, too. I like to think my mother's in heaven right now, and she's watching me."

"I'm sure she is," Phoebe said. She reached over to the bedside table and switched off the light. For a moment, there was silence in the darkness. Then Jessica spoke again.

"Fee?"

"Yeah?"

"I'm going to try not to be so shy any more."

Phoebe felt a warm tingle go through her. Maybe she really *was* helping Jessica.

Now, if only Ms Lacey knew it!

Chapter 6

The entire class stood in the front of the room, looking at the empty chairs and desks before them. Phoebe felt as if everyone was getting ready to perform for an invisible audience.

Of course, the seats wouldn't remain empty for long. Phoebe could think of several kids in the class who were notoriously bad spellers. They'd be going back to their seats after the first few words.

But they got an audience even before that. Mr Hoffmann came into the room.

"Good morning, boys and girls," he boomed in his hearty, principal's voice. "Ms Lacey, I understand your students are having a spelling bee this morning. May I observe?"

"Certainly," Ms Lacey replied. "We'd be delighted." Mr Hoffmann took a seat in the front of the room and gazed at the students expectantly.

Phoebe stole a glance at Jessica, way down at the end of the row. She was pale, but didn't look frightened. In fact, she wore a determined expression that Phoebe couldn't remember having seen before. She wasn't going to go down on the first word. Not this time.

Ms Lacey addressed the group. "Now, we've done this before, and you all know the rules. I'll give you a word, you repeat it, spell it, and say it again. If you miss a word, you'll have to sit down. Everyone understand?"

They nodded.

"Good," Ms Lacey said. "Then let's begin."

Gina Allston got the first word – *rational*. She had no problem with it. Ivan Fisher breezed through *predator*. The next person on line stumbled for a second on *emancipation*, but managed to recover and spell it correctly.

The first casualty was Robby.

"*Outrageous*," Ms Lacey told him.

Robby grinned. "How about if I act it out instead of spelling it?" He made one of those faces he thought was so funny.

Ms Lacey raised her eyes as if she was seeking assistance from the heavens. "No, Robby, you have to spell it. *Outrageous*."

Robby scratched his head. "*O-U-T-R-A-G-O-U-S*."

"That's incorrect," Ms Lacey said. "Take a seat."

"It's not fair," Robby complained. "I knew how to spell all those other words."

"It's the luck of the draw," Ms Lacey replied. "Now, please sit down." Her no-nonsense tone, combined with a meaningful glance at Mr Hoffmann, did the trick. Robby sat down.

Two more boys went down before it was Phoebe's turn.

"*Escalate*."

She was lucky – it was an easy one. Phoebe breathed a quick sigh of relief before she repeated the word and spelled it.

The spelling bee continued. Linn and Melanie made it through their words. Phoebe knew Melanie wouldn't last much longer – she was a terrible speller. And Linn hadn't practised at all.

Jessica was at the end of the line, and Phoebe held her breath as Ms Lacey approached her. Let her get an easy one, Phoebe prayed. Don't let her be the first girl down.

"*Deteriorate*."

It wasn't that easy, but it could have been worse. And Phoebe felt sure Jessica knew it. But would she stay cool, or would she lose her nerve and blow it?

There was only the slightest tremble in Jessica's voice as she repeated the word. And then she spelled it. Perfectly.

Phoebe wanted to cheer. Even Ms Lacey looked pleasantly surprised. "Absolutely correct," she said, giving Jessica a special smile.

The words went on, and they started getting harder. Melanie was the first girl to go down, but it didn't seem to bother her particularly. More girls followed rapidly.

Phoebe couldn't believe her luck with the next word – perceive. She remembered the "except after *c*" rule, and got the word right.

Students were dropping like flies. The boy on Jessica's right missed *devastation*. Jessica's voice was clear and calm as she spelled it correctly.

Very quickly, the seats in the room filled up. The words were coming at Phoebe faster and faster, but she held her ground. Amazingly, so did Jessica.

Phoebe couldn't believe her friend was still holding on.

And then there were only three spellers left – Phoebe, Jessica, and Ivan. The words flew by. Ivan got *capricious*. Phoebe spelled *parallel*. And Jessica didn't even falter on *monarchy*.

It was Ivan's turn again.

"*Changeable*."

Ivan responded promptly. "*C-H-A-N-G-A-B-L-E*."

"I'm sorry, Ivan," Ms Lacey said, in a more gentle voice than usual. "That was wrong."

Ivan just stood there for a second, his face registering disbelief. Then he sneered, as if he was expressing his contempt for the word. Finally, he sat down.

"Phoebe? *Changeable*."

Phoebe remembered the *e*. Then it was Jessica's turn.

Phoebe looked at her. Jessica's face was flushed slightly, and her eyes were bright. She wants to win, Phoebe thought. She really wants to win!

"*Demeanour*."

"*Demeanour*," Jessica repeated slowly, as if she were sounding it out. "*D-E-M-E-... N-O-R?*"

Phoebe's heart sank. It was a hard word. Of course, *she* knew it. She even remembered asking her father what it meant.

"That's incorrect." Ms Lacey's voice was soft with sympathy. "But don't sit down, Jessica. We have to see if Phoebe can spell it correctly first. If she misses it, you'll get a new word."

In the few seconds it took Ms Lacey to say this, a

million thoughts raced through Phoebe' head. Winning this spelling bee would mean a lot to Jessica. If Phoebe missed the word, Jessica would get another chance. She remembered what she and Linn and Melanie had pledged the night they visited Jessica – she'd vowed to think more about Jessica than herself.

"Phoebe," Ms Lacey said. " *Demeanour*."

And Phoebe knew what she had to do. Jessica *deserved* some glory. "*Demeanour*. D-E-M-E-E-N-E-R. *Demeanour*."

Ms Lacey looked at her in surprise. "That's incorrect. All right, Jessica, you get another chance. *Extraordinary*."

Wide-eyed, Jessica repeated the word. "*Extraordinary*. E-X-T-R-A-O-R-D-I-N-A-R-Y. *Extraordinary*."

Ms Lacey clapped her hands. "Correct! Take a bow, Jessica. You're the new class spelling champion!" She turned to the others. "How about a round of applause for Jessica?"

The class obliged. And as they applauded, Phoebe edged back to her own seat. Jessica remained in front of the class, her eyes shining, her face reflecting pride mixed with a little embarrassment at all the attention.

Phoebe wouldn't have been embarrassed. She would have loved every minute of it. And watching Mr Hoffmann shake Jessica's hand while Ms Lacey took a picture of them made her feel a twinge. It could have been her.

Still, she'd done the right thing, she assured herself. It was only a spelling bee. And Jessica needed this little boost. It was good for her to feel special. The glow on Jessica's face – she'd never seen her friend look like that. It was worth sacrificing the spelling bee.

But even so, when Ms Lacey reached in her desk drawer and pulled out a gold-coloured medal, Phoebe felt that twinge again. She hadn't known there was going to be a medal.

"I found this in an antique store," Ms Lacey said. "Some student won it in a spelling bee over fifty years ago."

Jessica gazed at it in awe. "Thank you," she gulped.

"Maybe you could put it on a chain and wear it round your neck," Ms Lacey suggested.

"She can have my ribbon," Gina Allston called out. She whipped a thin strip of black velvet out of her hair and brought it up to the front.

"That's very sweet of you, Gina," Ms Lacey said. She threaded the ribbon through the medal, and fastened it round Jessica's neck. Once again, the class applauded.

On the way to lunch, Linn couldn't shut up about Jessica. "She looks so happy! I still can't believe she pulled it off. She wasn't even nervous! Isn't it great?"

Phoebe nodded. "Great."

"Too bad you had to lose, though," Linn added.

Phoebe waved that aside. "It's not that big a deal."

"Ms Lacey's acting like it's a big deal," Linn said pointedly.

Phoebe shrugged it off. But all through lunch as the others chattered, Phoebe wondered about it. Not winning a stupid spelling bee really wasn't a big deal to her. But what sort of impression had she made on Ms Lacey? Had Phoebe blown her chance to appear on TV?

Of course, if Ms Lacey knew *why* she had lost, she'd be proud of Phoebe. She'd see Phoebe as a caring, sensitive person who was willing to sacrifice her own ambitions to make a friend happy.

And Jessica did look happy. She fingered the medal hanging round her neck. "I was so nervous! Did it show?"

"Hardly at all," Linn assured her.

"I couldn't believe it when you missed that word, Fee!" Jessica went on. "I was just taking a wild guess at it. I don't even know what *demeanour* means!"

"It's the way a person acts," Phoebe told her. "Like, if you're shy, that's your demeanour."

"I wasn't shy today," Jessica said in wonderment.

"You were terrific!" Melanie exclaimed. Linn reached across the table and patted Jessica's hand.

"And I'll bet your mother would have been very proud of you."

Jessica's eyes immediately filled with tears. But she was still smiling. "I think so, too."

I did the right thing, Phoebe thought. But she wished Ms Lacey knew.

She was leaving the cafeteria with her friends when Ivan came up to her.

"It looks like we have something in common," he said in his usual pompous way.

Phoebe looked desperately at her friends, but they had already walked on ahead, leaving her alone to face Ivan. "What are you talking about?"

"We both lost the spelling bee."

Phoebe shivered. She couldn't bear the thought that she had *anything* in common with Ivan. "There's a big difference. I lost on purpose."

Ivan actually looked startled. "What do you mean?"

Phoebe eyed him haughtily. "I knew perfectly well how to spell that word. I misspelled it on purpose so Jessica could win."

Ivan stared at her. "What did you do that for?"

Phoebe felt terribly noble. "In case you haven't heard, Jessica's mother just died. I thought winning the spelling bee might make her feel better. I wanted to do something special for my friend."

Ivan's upper lip curled in a particularly nasty way. "That's stupid. I wouldn't have done that."

"I believe it," Phoebe snapped. "Because you don't have any friends."

It was an awful thing to say to a person, but it was true. And Ivan didn't seem the least bit dismayed. He just shook his head sadly, as if Phoebe had disappointed him. Phoebe tossed her head and marched away.

If her image had fallen in Ivan's eyes, well, she couldn't care less. But for the rest of the afternoon, she watched Ms Lacey carefully. Did the teacher think less of her now?

It was hard to say. Phoebe tried not to worry about it. But it was impossible. And when class was dismissed that afternoon, she dawdled at her desk until everyone had left. She'd be late for hall duty, but this was more important.

"Uh, Ms Lacey?"

The teacher was busily straightening up her desk and barely glanced at her. "Yes, Phoebe?"

"It's about the spelling bee."

"Now, Phoebe, there's no shame in coming second. You can't win all the time."

"But I could have won," Phoebe persisted. "I knew how to spell that word. I misspelled it on purpose."

The teacher looked at her strangely. "Phoebe, you don't have to make up an excuse like that."

"But I'm not making it up! Honestly, Ms Lacey, I lost on purpose so Jessica could have a chance to win."

Ms Lacey was still looking at her in that odd way, and Phoebe hastened to explain. "See, I thought it might make her feel better if she won something."

Still Ms Lacey didn't smile. "If what you're telling me is true, Phoebe . . ."

"It is!" Phoebe insisted.

"Then I'm not sure what to say." Ms Lacey paused for a minute. Phoebe couldn't tell what the expression on her face meant. But this much she knew: it definitely wasn't approval.

"I'm sure you thought you were helping Jessica," Ms Lacey said. "But losing on purpose like that – it's cheating, in a sense. What you've done is deprive another person of the chance to earn something on her own. Do you understand what I'm saying?"

Phoebe wasn't sure. All she understood was that Ms Lacey wasn't happy with her.

"That's not the way to help a friend, Phoebe." Ms

Lacey returned to gathering up papers on her desk. "Now, we'll just have to pretend this never happened. I hope you're not planning to tell Jessica what you did. I know it would upset her to think she hadn't won on her own."

Phoebe felt numb, but she managed to shake her head.

"And I hope you won't do anything so foolish again."

Phoebe nodded. And since there seemed to be nothing more to say, she left the room.

There was coconut cake for dessert that evening. Phoebe hated anything with coconut in it. But it was Jessica's favourite. When Mrs Gray learned that Jessica had won the spelling bee, she asked Jessica what her favourite dessert was. And then she immediately set about making a coconut cake, even though she knew Phoebe didn't like it.

But Phoebe didn't say a word about it. All through dinner, she kept a fixed smile on her face while Jessica recounted the details of her triumph. Phoebe didn't even make a face when her mother, with a brief apologetic glance at her, brought the cake to the table. Carefully, she pushed at her slice of cake with her fork, trying to pick out pieces that didn't have the tiniest bit of coconut on them.

At least she was keeping the vow she'd made. She was putting Jessica before herself. Too bad no one else seemed to appreciate it.

"I'm trying not to be so shy," Jessica was saying.

Daphne sympathized. "I know that's not easy."

Cassie cocked her head to one side and examined Jessica thoughtfully. "You know what might help? A whole new look."

"Good grief," Lydia muttered.

Jessica looked at her uneasily. "What do you mean?"

"A new hairstyle," Cassie announced, "and different clothes. You've got nice hair, but wearing it long and straight like that is boring."

"Cassie!" Mrs Gray exclaimed. "It's not very nice to call someone's hair boring."

Jessica was tugging on a lock of her hair. She actually seemed concerned.

"Ignore her," Phoebe advised. "There's nothing wrong with your hair."

"How can hair be boring, anyway?" Mr Gray asked. He turned to his wife. "Is my hair boring?"

Mrs Gray looked at him critically. "Actually, I don't think there's enough of it to be able to tell."

Cassie glared at them in exasperation. "Okay, go ahead and make fun of me. But this is what they've been teaching us at the Teen Board meetings at Benson's. Hair can be interesting, or it can be boring. No offence, Jessica, but your hair's boring."

Phoebe wanted to strangle her. "Knock it off, Cassie! Don't you think Jessica's got more important things to think about than her hair?"

But Jessica was looking at Cassie with interest. "What could I do to make my hair more interesting?"

"You could dye it pink," Lydia suggested. "A girl in my science class did that. It's definitely interesting."

"I doubt her parents think so," Mrs Gray noted drily. "Jessica, please don't dye your hair. Your father would never forgive us."

"She doesn't need to dye it," Cassie said firmly. "Maybe tomorrow after school we could try something."

"Okay," Jessica said. Phoebe looked at her in surprise. Jessica sounded enthusiastic. For some strange reason, Phoebe felt that funny disgruntled twinge again. Cassie never offered to do anything with *her* hair – at least, not since the night Phoebe had been getting ready to speak at the town council. Not, of course, that she'd want her to. But still . . .

"Can we get off the subject of hair?" Lydia requested. "I've got a *real* problem, and I could use some advice."

"What kind of problem?" Mr Gray asked.

"You know the annual Field Day we have in May?"

Cassie wrinkled her nose. "You mean when they have those relay races?"

"It's more than relay races. It's all kinds of sports, like a mini-Olympics. Anyway, the Student Council picks a chairperson from the ninth grade to run it. And Martha Jane wants to use my influence to get her chosen."

"What's the problem?" Phoebe asked. "Martha Jane's a big athelete, right?"

"Oh, sure," Lydia said. "But the chairperson doesn't have to be a great athlete, just someone who's good at organizing and running things." She shook her head ruefully. "And that's *not* Martha Jane. She's always getting confused and losing things."

"And you feel she wouldn't be able to do a good job," Mr Gray commented.

Lydia nodded. "How can I support her in Student Council when I've been working with her on the *Alternative* all year and I know how she forgets things?"

"Have you tried talking to her about it?" Mrs Gray asked.

"No, not yet. I suppose I've been scared. I'm afraid she's going to be furious with me."

"That would be awful," Daphne murmured. "I'm glad I don't have to make a decision like that."

"Wait a minute," Phoebe said suddenly. "Martha Jane's your best friend, right?"

"Right."

"Then you should support her."

"But she's not the right person for it," Lydia objected.

"You could help her," Phoebe suggested. "You can't go against your best friend."

"Hold on," Mr Gray said. "Sometimes you can't let friendships affect your decisions, Fee."

"Sure you can," Phoebe insisted. "Personally, I think friends are more important than relay races."

"What do you think, Jessica?" Lydia asked.

"I don't know," Jessica admitted. She pushed a lock of her boring hair behind an ear. "But friends are awfully important. I know I'm lucky to have a friend like Fee."

Phoebe turned and smiled at her. Her eye caught

83

the glint of the gold medal round Jessica's neck, but she kept smiling.

And then she went back to picking the coconut out of her cake.

Chapter 7

"How does my hair look?" Jessica asked anxiously.

Phoebe sighed heavily. It was the third time that morning Jessica had asked the question. "It's fine," she said shortly.

Actually, she had to admit Jessica's hair looked better than fine. Cassie had outdone herself. She'd cut a long, tapered fringe that framed and softened Jessica's narrow face. The scraggly ends were trimmed. And Cassie had pulled Jessica's hair back, anchoring it on both sides with simple tortoiseshell combs. It was a definite improvement.

If Phoebe didn't show sufficient enthusiasm for Jessica's new look, Linn and Melanie more than made up for it when they all met in the hallway before class.

"Jess!" Melanie shrieked. "You look *fabulous*!"

"It's a whole new look!" Linn exclaimed. "It's so elegant!"

Jessica giggled inelegantly, but twirled round so they could admire her hairdo from all angles. When the uproar died down, Linn reached into her purse and pulled out a handful of envelopes.

"What are those?" Phoebe asked.

"Valentines, dummy," Linn replied. "It's Valentine's Day, remember?"

Phoebe looked at her in alarm. "But Ms Lacey

doesn't approve of giving out valentines. That's why I didn't bring any."

"She just said it's not nice if you're not giving them to everyone," Linn corrected her. "But I know some of the kids brought them anyway, and they're going to slip them in people's desks when Ms Lacey isn't looking."

"Well, I don't want to do anything that might get me into any trouble," Phoebe announced, but no one was listening. They'd started talking about Jessica's hair again.

And when they moved into the classroom, Ms Lacey noticed it too. "Jessica, you look lovely."

"Thank you, Ms Lacey." Phoebe noticed that Jessica didn't turn nearly as pink as usual when the teacher spoke to her. Phoebe smoothed the front of her red jumper, a Daphne hand-me-down. She'd taken extra pains with her own appearance that morning. But Ms Lacey didn't comment on it.

Oh well, Phoebe told herself for the umpteenth time, Jessica needed special attention. As they headed for their seats, she said, "You really do look different. Not that you looked bad before."

"I *feel* different," Jessica confided. "You know, Cassie was right. A little thing like this can make a person feel more sure of herself."

It showed. That morning, Ms Lacey was showing a film. When she turned on the projector, there was sound but no picture.

"It looks like the bulb's burnt out. Would someone like to go to the office and get us a new one?"

Several hands, including Phoebe's, shot up. But Ms

Lacey was not looking at any of them. Phoebe followed the teacher's eyes and realized she was looking at Jessica.

Jessica had actually put up her hand. It wasn't very high, but it was definitely up. Phoebe was floored. She'd never seen Jessica volunteer to run an errand at school. Running an errand meant talking to strangers, something Jessica always avoided.

"Jessica? Would you get a bulb for us?"

Jessica nodded. Slowly, she got up. Then, head raised, shoulders back, and looking like a soldier going into battle, she marched out of the room.

"While we're waiting for Jessica," Ms Lacey said, "I want to say something to you all about Valentine's Day. I'm sure that, despite my advice, some of you are absolutely determined to exchange valentines. All I ask is that you exchange them quietly and unobtrusively. Perhaps you could slip them in your friends' desks at lunch time."

Phoebe was dismayed to see several kids nodding. Great, she thought. Now if she didn't get any, she'd feel bad. And if she did, she'd still feel bad for not giving out any.

A few minutes later, Jessica returned and handed a new bulb to Ms Lacey.

"Very good," Ms Lacey said. "Thank you, Jessica. We appreciate your getting this for us."

She certainly was making a big deal out of it, Phoebe thought. You'd think Jessica had just given her a million dollars instead of a crummy light bulb.

Later, just before lunch, Ms Lacey announced that

she wanted to talk about the television documentary. Phoebe sat up straight and listened intently.

"I still don't know much more about it," she told them. "And I suspect we won't know any details until the television people arrive. We've been told that they don't want us to prepare at all. But as I mentioned before, they do want us to select a sixth-grade student for a brief interview, and Mr Hoffmann has asked me to pick someone from this class."

Phoebe watched her anxiously. Ms Lacey wasn't looking at her. But then, she wasn't looking directly at anyone in particular.

"During lunch, I want you to think about whom you would like to have representing you on television. When you come back, I'll hear your suggestions. Feel free to nominate yourself if you like. Then I'll have the weekend to think it over, and on Monday I'll tell you my decision."

Phoebe didn't want to nominate herself. Despite what Ms Lacey had said, it seemed like a conceited thing to do. Over lunch, she talked to the others about it. "One of you three nominate me, okay?"

"I'll do it," Jessica offered instantly.

"Okay," Phoebe replied. "Thanks."

Jessica smiled happily. "You know, running that errand wasn't so bad. But I got a little nervous when I went in the office and saw Mrs Powell in there."

Melanie's eyes grew large. "The assistant principal? Yuck! She's so scary!"

"No kidding," Jessica said. "The minute I walked in, she looked at me like I was on the Ten Most

Wanted list. And when she said, 'What are you doing out of class?' I almost burst into tears."

"What did you say?" Linn asked.

"At first I couldn't say anything," Jessica confessed. "Then I remembered something my mother used to tell me. She said whenever people frightened me, I should try to imagine what they looked like in their underwear."

Melanie burst into laughter. "Mrs Powell in her underwear! Gross!"

Jessica nodded fervently. "But thinking about that made her a whole lot less scary. So I just told her why I was there, and she gave me a bulb."

"That's great!" Linn declared. "Congratulations!"

Jessica looked terribly proud of herself. Phoebe thought about the zillions of errands *she'd* run for Ms Lacey.

"I want to get some more milk," Melanie announced.

"Me too," Jessica said. "Let me go and get it."

"You'll have to ask the cafeteria lady for it," Melanie warned. "Sometimes she's not very nice about it."

"I can do it," Jessica insisted. "I need the practice."

After she left the table, Linn turned to the others, her eyes glowing. "Isn't this wonderful? Jessica's like a whole new person. She's talking to people, she's volunteering, she won the spelling bee – "

"I let her win," Phoebe blurted out. She hadn't meant to tell them. But she deserved a little credit.

"You're kidding!" Melanie exclaimed.

"No, I'm not kidding," Phoebe replied. "I could

tell she really wanted to win, and I knew it would make her feel better about herself. So I misspelled that word on purpose."

She was pleased to see how impressed both Melanie and Linn appeared.

"Wow," Melanie remarked in awe, "you gave up the chance to win just to make Jessica feel good."

"That was really, really nice of you," Linn said, and the sincerity in her voice was unmistakable.

"It was nothing," Phoebe said, feeling terribly noble and virtuous. "Like I said before, we should be thinking of her more than ourselves. She needs her friends to help her right now."

"You're a real friend," Linn proclaimed. Then she sighed regretfully. "I haven't done anything at all to help Jessica. You're the one who's making sacrifices."

"I just don't want to be selfish," Phoebe explained. She was enjoying the role of the one, true friend. "Jessica needs good things to happen to her right now more than I do."

Linn looked at her thoughtfully. "And you really didn't mind losing the spelling bee."

Phoebe shook her head. "I don't mind giving up something if it's going to make Jessica feel better about herself. That's what friends are for."

Jessica returned with the milk, and the next few minutes were taken up with her report on this latest accomplishment.

"I want to get back to class early to see if I got any valentines," Melanie said, gulping the last of her milk.

"I've already put mine in your desks," Linn said.

The girls trooped back to their room. Gina Allston

was there, furtively opening desks. "My mother made me buy them for everyone," she explained.

Phoebe hoped the whole class hadn't done the same. When she opened her own desk top, she found three. One was from Gina, and one was from Linn. When she opened the third, she smiled happily. It was a standard hearts-and-flowers valentine, but it was signed "To one of my favourite students, Best wishes, Ms Lacey."

"Look what I got," she cried gleefully. Her smile faded when she saw an identical card on Linn's desk.

"I guess she gave one to everyone," Linn said. Phoebe examined the inscription on Linn's card. It was exactly the same.

"Jess, did you get a card from Ms Lacey?" Phoebe asked.

"I'm not sure." Jessica was looking a little dazed. She had her desk top open, and Phoebe gasped when she saw what was inside. Jessica must have had at least a dozen valentines.

"Wow," Linn said respectfully. "You're getting awfully popular."

Everyone just feels sorry for her, Phoebe thought, and then she felt ashamed. She shouldn't be jealous of poor Jessica.

Within the next few minutes, the rest of the class returned, and then Ms Lacey came back. She stood in front of the class with a pad in her hand.

"I hope you've all had a chance to think about the documentary. I'd like to hear your suggestions for a spokesperson."

Robby Cooper's hand shot up. "Me!"

"All right, Robby," Ms Lacey said, and jotted his name down on her pad.

Then Elizabeth Fine nominated Deirdre Callahan, and Deirdre Callahan nominated Elizabeth Fine. Phoebe considered their chances. Liz made good grades, but she never said much in class. And Deirdre was the type who was always bursting into tears over nothing.

Phoebe focused her attention on Jessica. Finally, Jessica raised her hand. It wasn't much of a gesture – her hand barely reached the top of her head. But Ms Lacey saw it.

"Yes, Jessica?"

"I want to nominate Phoebe."

"Thank you, Jessica. Any more?"

Ivan raised his hand. "I'd like to suggest myself."

He doesn't have a chance, Phoebe thought. So far, so good.

And then Linn raised her hand. Phoebe looked at her, puzzled. Hadn't she heard Jessica's nomination?

"Yes, Linn?"

"I'd like to nominate Jessica."

Phoebe's mouth fell open. What was the matter with Linn? Had she gone crazy? Jessica simply looked stunned.

Ms Lacey thanked Linn and asked if there were any more suggestions. When there weren't, she instructed the class to open their social studies books.

The afternoon went by in a blur. A zillion feelings were racing through Phoebe. She was angry, she was hurt, she was bewildered. How could Linn do this to her? Didn't she realize how much being on TV meant to her?

She wanted to confront Linn in gym, but her friend's group was on the mats and her own was on the other side of the room, climbing ropes. And their lockers weren't near each other.

It wasn't until the class was getting ready for the Valentine's Day party that Phoebe was able to corner Linn.

"Why did you do that? Why did you nominate Jessica?" She kept her voice low so Ms Lacey wouldn't hear, but the anger must have shown on her face, because Linn looked alarmed.

"I thought you'd be pleased."

"Pleased! Are you nuts?"

Now Linn looked defensive. "You were the one who said you didn't mind giving something up for Jessica. And this would be so great for her."

"Phoebe!" Ms Lacey called. "Could you help put out these cupcakes?"

Phoebe threw Linn one last withering glance and stalked off to help Ms Lacey. As the party got going, she forced herself to calm down. She didn't want her anger to show. And she didn't want to take it out on Jessica, either. After all, it wasn't her fault that Linn had done something so stupid.

And the more she thought about it, the less worried she became. It wasn't as if Jessica really had a chance. Ms Lacey might be feeling sorry for her, but she wouldn't risk putting a notoriously tongue-tied person on TV. True, Jessica wasn't as shy as she'd been. But she wasn't ready for television. Not by a long shot.

Phoebe was on her way to the front of the room for another cupcake when Ivan came up to her.

"Congratulations."

"For what?" Phoebe asked.

"I have a pretty good suspicion Ms Lacey is going to choose you for the TV show."

Phoebe tried to sound casual. "What makes you think that?"

"Because she likes you."

"That won't have anything to do with her decision," Phoebe said primly. "Ms Lacey will pick the person who's best qualified."

"Then you'll still get it," Ivan said. "Next to me, you're the best qualified."

It was a compliment – sort of. Naturally, Ivan thought he was the best. But even so, Phoebe had never heard him give anyone a compliment before, "Thanks," she said cautiously. "But if you're so well qualified, maybe she'll pick you."

"I doubt it," Ivan said. "She doesn't like me."

"Don't be silly," Phoebe protested without much conviction. "Ms Lacey likes everyone."

"Oh, I don't care if she doesn't like me," Ivan said. "I don't like her either. I think she's a crummy teacher."

Phoebe was indignant. "She is not!"

Ivan went on as if she hadn't even spoken. "In fact, I was thinking of complaining to my parents about her. Maybe they could get her fired."

Phoebe rolled her eyes and threw up her hands.

There was no point in trying to be nice to Ivan. He was just basically unlikable. She'd never understand him. How could a person not have any friends? He didn't even seem to want any.

She wondered why. Ivan was a total mystery to her. Maybe one day she'd play detective and try to find out what made him the way he was. But right now, she had more important things on her mind.

She got her cupcake and went over to Ms Lacey.

"Would you like some help cleaning up after class?" she asked. "I don't have hall duty this afternoon."

Ms Lacey glanced at the clock. "Oh, my goodness – it's almost time for the bell. Yes, Phoebe, I'd like some help very much."

Phoebe beamed. Now she'd have a chance to talk to Ms Lacey alone. But the teacher's next words dispelled that notion.

"I have to go directly to a faculty meeting. But all you need to do is collect the rubbish and throw it away. And straighten up the chairs if you have a chance."

The bell rang and everyone began scrambling round, gathering books and coats. The room was a disaster – chairs had been pushed every which way, the remains of cupcakes were all over the desks, and crumpled napkins littered the floor.

Phoebe saw Jessica and Melanie and Linn waiting by the door. They were huddled together, whispering. When Phoebe went up to them, they stopped abruptly. She had a pretty good idea whom they were talking about.

"I'm staying to help clean up," she told them. "You lot go on without me."

Jessica was looking at her anxiously, and Phoebe knew why. Linn must have told her she was angry. She forced a reassuring smile. "If Mom's home, tell her I'll be a little late, okay?"

Relief flooded Jessica's face. "Okay," she said. "I'll see you later."

Phoebe went back to survey the mess she was now obliged to clean up.

It had started snowing. Not one of the nice, soft, light snows Phoebe liked, but a wet snow, the kind that penetrated the thickest boots. By the time Phoebe reached home, she was cold, wet, and hungry.

And she was still thinking about the TV show. She kept reminding herself that what Linn had done wouldn't hurt her own chances. Ivan was right, for once. Ms Lacey did like her. And she was definitely the most qualified of all the kids nominated.

She hoped Jessica wouldn't be hurt when she wasn't chosen. But Jess probably didn't want to do it anyway. Facing the assistant principal was one thing. Facing a TV camera was another thing altogether.

The house was silent. Phoebe hung up her coat, pulled off her boots, and went to the refrigerator to check out potential snacks. Under a ladybird magnet on the door was a note from Lydia. "Took Jessica to a film. Back at six."

Just then, her mother came in through the kitchen door. "Hi, sweetie. Oooh, it's cold out there."

"Mom, look at this."

Her mother glanced at the note. "What about it?"

"Lydia promised to take *me* to a film the next time she had passes!"

Mrs Gray sat down at the kitchen table and began tugging off her boots. "Were you here when they left?"

"No, I stayed after school to clean up after our party."

"Then she couldn't have taken you anyway."

What her mother said made perfectly good sense, but Phoebe wasn't satisfied. "Well, Lydia should have told me about it yesterday. I could have been here if I had known she had passes."

The outrage in her voice had an impact. Mrs Gray gazed at her quizzically. "Fee, it's just a film. And don't you think Jessica deserves a little treat? She's been through a lot. Surely you don't mind giving up one little film so that Jessica can go."

Phoebe was in no mood to hear another lecture about making sacrifices for Jessica. "Okay, okay, forget it." She opened the refrigerator. "Is there anything to eat?"

"Wait a minute, Fee." Her mother was looking at her seriously. "I hope you do realize how much Jessica has suffered. I'd like to think you'd be willing to make a few sacrifices – "

"But I have!" Phoebe interrupted hotly. "I've been making tons of sacrifices!" She stopped suddenly. She was on the verge of telling her mother about the spelling bee. But she had a feeling her mother wouldn't approve any more than Ms Lacey had. Grown-ups tended to agree about things like that.

"Fee, are you upset about something?"

"No," Phoebe replied firmly. "I'm just hungry." She went back to her exploration of the refrigerator's contents.

"Don't spoil your appetite," Mrs Gray said. "I was thinking that we should all go out for dinner tonight."

Phoebe brightened. "Can we go to El Diablo?" The Mexican restaurant was her favourite.

"That sounds like a good idea. I'll see what your father says."

Considering that her father was a serious guacamole freak, Phoebe decided she could pretty much count on El Diablo. And a couple of tacos would definitely take the sting out of missing a film.

She went up to her room and started on her homework. She made it through her maths problems and then attacked her social studies reading. It was hard to concentrate, though. She kept having fantasies about the TV show. And not just the show itself, but what could happen because of it. She might become famous! Maybe she could have her own kids talk show, with singing and dancing and celebrities. Scenes played themselves out in her head – "*The Kids' Show,*" *starring Phoebe Gray! Tonight, Phoebe interviews Michael Jackson!*

She was so caught up in her daydreams that she was only vaguely aware of hearing Lydia and Jessica downstairs. A few minutes later, Jessica appeared in the room.

"Hi." Once again, she was eyeing Phoebe uneasily, as if unsure of her reception.

But the fantasies had put Phoebe in a good mood, and she greeted Jessica kindly. "How was the film?"

Jessica made a face. "Not too good. It was about this teenager who was really unpopular at school. He sort of reminded me of Ivan Fisher. Anyway, he gets really angry because none of the girls will go to a dance with him, so he turns into a monster and he starts killing them all. It was pretty horrid."

Phoebe loved that kind of film. But she kept the regret off her face. "Well, at least it was free."

Jessica sat down on the bed. "Linn thinks you're angry that she nominated me for that TV thing."

"Oh, I'm not angry," Phoebe said quickly. "I was just surprised, that's all. Because she didn't tell me she was going to do it."

"Then you don't mind?" Jessica asked hopefully.

Phoebe shook her head.

"Good," Jessica said with relief. "I mean, it's not as if Ms Lacey would ever pick me anyway."

"Would you want to do it if she did?" Phoebe asked.

She expected Jessica to look horrified at the mere suggestion. Instead, she looked pensive.

"Probably not," she said slowly. There was a moment of silence. "Do you want me to drop out? I mean, I could tell Ms Lacey I'm not interested in doing it."

"Oh, you don't have to do that," Phoebe replied generously. "Like you said, it's not as if you really have a chance." That didn't sound very nice, she decided. "I mean, you have a *chance*, but I think she might pick me."

Jessica agreed. "I think so, too."

"You won't be hurt if she picks me, will you?"

Jessica shook her head. "I think I had better change my clothes if we're going out to dinner."

Phoebe heard her father downstairs. "I'll be back straight away."

She ran downstairs and found her father in the kitchen with her mother. "What time are we going to El Diablo?" she asked.

"Honey, we're going to the Chinese restaurant instead," her mother told her. "Jessica doesn't like Mexican food."

Phoebe groaned. Chinese food wasn't bad. But she'd had her heart set on El Diablo.

"Now don't start whining, Fee," her father admonished her. "We can go to El Diablo another time. And Jessica – "

"I know, I know," Phoebe interrupted. "We have to be especially nice to her." She swallowed her disappointment. "Chinese food is okay. If that's what Jessica wants."

"That's my girl," Mr Gray said. "I knew you wouldn't really mind making a little sacrifice for your friend."

Phoebe nodded, and ambled out of the room. *Don't be selfish*, she told herself. *You can give up a taco for your friend. It's no big deal.*

But even as she tried to convince herself, she couldn't help but wonder how many more of these little sacrifices she was going to have to make for Jessica.

Chapter 8

On Monday morning, it wasn't easy for Phoebe to open her eyes. She hadn't slept very well. Or maybe she had, but her dreams had been so wild and crazy that she'd woken up exhausted.

She rolled over and faced the other twin bed. Daphne was sitting up and rubbing her eyes.

"Aren't you glad to be back in your own bed?" Phoebe asked.

"Mmmm." Daphne swung her legs over the side and got up. "Of course, I didn't mind giving it up for Jessica. She needed to be with a good friend like you." She slid into her slippers and padded out to the bathroom.

Sometimes Daphne could be too good for words, Phoebe thought. Jessica was great and all that and it had been okay having her there. But to be perfectly honest, Phoebe wasn't sorry Jessica's father had returned over the weekend and taken her home. With all the fuss everyone had been making over her friend, Phoebe was beginning to feel very unimportant. Almost invisible.

But none of this really mattered any more. She wouldn't be invisible much longer. Certainly not after Ms Lacey made her announcement.

She wondered if she should wear something especially nice that day. No, it would only look as if she were *expecting* to be chosen. But she did choose some nice corduroy trousers instead of jeans, and a bright yellow sweater.

In the kitchen, Lydia was talking to their mother. "We've got Student Council this afternoon. And I have to decide whether or not I'm going to recommend Martha Jane to be in charge of Field Day."

Mrs Gray handed Phoebe a box of cereal as she replied. "I know it's a hard decision, honey. But no one can make it for you. You'll have to do what you think is best."

Lydia groaned, and Phoebe could sympathize. Their parents were *always* saying things like that. Sometimes asking for their advice was a total waste of time. She studied the picture of the film star on the cereal box and thought about how she'd pose for her own photograph.

"Mom," she said, "can we go out to dinner at El Diablo tonight?"

Her mother looked doubtful. "I don't think so, Fee. You know your father's always especially tired on Monday nights."

"Okay," Phoebe said agreeably. "Then can we have something special for dinner tonight? Like fried chicken, maybe?"

"Maybe," Mrs Gray said. "If I get a chance to stop at the market. What's the occasion?"

Phoebe gazed up at the ceiling. "Oh, there might be something to celebrate."

Her mother looked at her with interest, but Phoebe just smiled mysteriously. "I'll tell you about it later. You know, I think I'll walk to school today."

Now her mother really looked curious. Phoebe never walked when she could ride. She drummed up a half-baked excuse. "I need the exercise." Mainly, she wanted to avoid her mother's questions. She was afraid she'd end up blurting out the whole thing.

And it *was* a nice day for walking – cold, but the sun was shining. She felt like skipping, but she didn't because she had to watch for ice patches. In her mind, though, she was dancing all the way to school.

She had a lot to feel good about. Somehow, she just knew Ms Lacey was going to pick her for the TV show. There wasn't any real competition. And she felt pretty sure Jessica wouldn't be upset about it.

Jessica was another reason to feel good. She was getting so much more sure of herself, like she was coming out of a shell – a shell Phoebe had helped her to crack. Even if she didn't get any credit for it, Phoebe knew she'd been a good friend to Jessica.

Entering school, she felt light and upbeat and full of anticipation. After cheerfully greeting Linn and Melanie, she breezed through hall duty. She was in such a good mood, she didn't even yell at two particularly obnoxious third graders who were balancing three ring-binders on their heads.

Then she went into class, and she started feeling a little jittery. She had expected Ms Lacey to make the announcement first thing. But she didn't. She acted as though it was just another ordinary day.

And for Phoebe, it became an especially long day. By lunch time, she felt like jumping out of her skin. But she tried to hide her feelings from the others. She didn't think it would be polite to talk about the TV show in front of Jessica.

"It must be nice having your dad back," she said to her.

Jessica nodded. "We've been having long talks. We never used to talk much before. And he says my Aunt Lucy is going to come and stay with us for a while."

"Is that the aunt who visited last Christmas?" Melanie asked.

"The one with the great clothes?" Linn added.

"Yeah, she's my father's sister. And she's lots of fun. It'll be like having my own sister." She smiled shyly at Phoebe. "When I was staying with you, it was like having sisters. It felt good."

Her smile was full of affection. Phoebe hoped her friend would feel the same after Ms Lacey made the announcement. But she wasn't too worried about it. Even something as important as being on TV shouldn't come between good friends.

The afternoon went by as slowly as the morning. Ms Lacey didn't mention the television show. Was it possible she had forgotten? It was all Phoebe could do to keep from asking her.

Luckily, Ivan didn't have her self-control. Twenty minutes before the bell, he raised his hand. "Ms Lacey, have you decided who's going to be on the television documentary?"

"Yes, I have, Ivan. But I wanted to wait until the end of the day before I made the announcement."

Ivan made a big show of checking his watch, and

then looking at the clock above the blackboard. "It's just twenty minutes before the bell."

Ms Lacey sighed. "All right. First of all, I want to tell you that this was a very difficult decision for me to make. Any one of you would have done an excellent job representing this class. But the television people want only one person." She paused. "And that person will be Jessica Duncan."

Phoebe was dimly aware of applause and someone yelling "All right, Jessica!" Ms Lacey was still talking, but Phoebe was too stunned to hear what she was saying.

Jessica . . . how could that be? It was impossible! This was supposed to be Phoebe's job. It was going to be her chance to shine again. She'd counted on it. She'd planned for it, she'd dreamed about it – it meant everything to her! How could Ms Lacey do this to her?

Jessica . . . it was all wrong! Jessica didn't deserve it. She had been talking a little, volunteering a little – big deal! And just because her mother had died didn't mean they all had to go giving her special treatment for ever! It wasn't fair – it just wasn't fair!

When the bell rang, Phoebe sat in her seat, waiting for the room to empty. Then she got up and went to the teacher's desk.

"Ms Lacey . . ."

"Yes, Phoebe?" Her eyes were kind, and her expression was sympathetic. That didn't make Phoebe feel the least bit better.

There was no point in beating around the bush.

She didn't worry about impressing Ms Lacey any more. "Why did you pick Jessica?"

"Because I think she'll do a good job," Ms Lacey said promptly.

"But she won't!" Phoebe said passionately. "She's too shy, and too nervous, and she gets flustered when people look at her! She's just not qualified!"

Ms Lacey raised her eyebrows. "There aren't any particular qualifications for this job, Phoebe. And surely you've noticed that Jessica is working very hard to overcome her shyness. I think this will be a great opportunity for her to develop more self-confidence." She put a hand on Phoebe's shoulder. "I know you wanted to do this, Phoebe. And I'm sure you would have done a fine job. But I wish you could be happy for your friend."

Phoebe wanted to explode. *Be happy for your friend. Make sacrifices for your friend. Give up everything for your friend.*

Ms Lacey was looking at her steadily. "Now, I'd like to believe that you're just trying to protect Jessica. I don't want to think you're selfish and insensitive to Jessica's needs."

What about *my* needs? Phoebe wanted to cry. Don't *I* matter any more? But there was no point in saying anything at all. Ms Lacey didn't understand.

She went back to her desk, got her books, retrieved her coat, and left the room.

At first, she thought the hall was deserted. Then she saw Jessica, standing in the shadows.

"Fee, do you hate me?" Jessica's voice was soft and

pitiful. "Do you want me to tell Ms Lacey I don't want to do it?"

Phoebe couldn't meet her eyes. "Do what you want. I don't really care." Without another word, she headed for the door. She was in absolutely no mood for hall duty.

As she walked home, she counted the people she hated. She hated Jessica for stealing the glory that was rightfully hers. She hated Linn for nominating Jessica. She hated Ms Lacey for choosing her. She hated everyone in the class for applauding.

Luckily, no one was home when she got there. She went straight to her bedroom, slammed the door, and curled up on her bed. She didn't cry, though. She couldn't. All she wanted to do was to lie there quietly and hate everybody.

She wasn't able to brood for long. A few minutes later, Daphne came in. She took one look at Phoebe's figure huddled on the bed and sat down on the edge next to her.

"Fee, what's the matter?"

Thank goodness Daphne was the only one she'd told. Of all her sisters, Daphne was the most understanding.

"Ms Lacey didn't pick me to be on TV."

Daphne promptly threw her arms round Phoebe and hugged her tightly. "Oh, Fee – I'm so sorry. I know you wanted this a lot."

She barely felt Daphne's embrace. It was as if her whole body was numb.

Finally, Daphne released her. "Who did she pick?"

"Jessica."

"Oh."

Phoebe didn't like the sound of that "oh". It wasn't a sympathetic "oh". It was more like an interested "oh". She fixed her eyes on her sister. "What do you mean, 'oh'?"

"Well, if it's not going to be you, at least it's someone you care about."

"What difference does *that* make?"

"It's nice for Jessica. And she needs—"

Phoebe didn't let her finish. "I'm sick of hearing what Jessica needs!" She got up and stormed out of the room.

But where was she going to go? Downstairs, she could hear her mother in the kitchen. She couldn't go there. Her mother could always tell from Phoebe's face when something was wrong. And if Phoebe told her, she'd just get another lecture on Jessica's needs.

She heard voices coming from the room Cassie and Lydia shared. The door was slightly open, so she went in.

"What's going on?" she asked, trying to make her voice sound as normal as possible.

Cassie was in her usual position, sitting at her dressing table and staring into the mirror. Lydia was sprawled on her bed, looking grim. "I was telling Cassie about the Student Council meeting. We picked the director for Field Day."

Phoebe remembered the conversation at the dinner table. "Did you pick Martha Jane?"

"No."

Cassie turned away from her reflection. "She's

going to be furious with you when she finds out. And I don't blame her."

"I know," Lydia moaned. "But I *couldn't* recommend her. She just doesn't have the right qualifications." She sat up and shot a warning at Phoebe. "And don't start telling me I should have put our friendship first. I feel bad enough about this already."

Phoebe shrugged. "I wasn't going to say that. Personally, I think you did the right thing."

Lydia looked startled. "You do? Boy, you've certainly changed your tune."

"I think you should always pick the person who's best for the job," Phoebe stated flatly. "Not just someone you feel sorry for."

"What are you talking about? I don't feel sorry for Martha Jane."

"Nothing," Phoebe muttered. "Never mind."

Cassie started talking about her Teen Board classes, a subject Phoebe found uninteresting. She wandered out of the room.

Well, since neither of them had noticed anything wrong with her, maybe her mother wouldn't either. Phoebe went down to the kitchen.

"Hi, honey," her mother greeted her. And then she clapped a hand to her forehead. "Oh, no – I forgot. You wanted fried chicken for dinner, right? And I forgot to stop at the market. I suppose I could run over there now."

"Don't bother," Phoebe said. "I'm not in the mood for fried chicken any more."

"Well, I've got lasagne in the freezer," her mother began, and then she stopped. She looked at Phoebe closely. "I thought you wanted something special tonight."

The phone rang, and as Mrs Gray went to answer it, Phoebe used the interruption to get out of the room before there could be any more questions.

She didn't want fried chicken. Fried chicken was for celebrations. And there was definitely, positively nothing for Phoebe to celebrate.

Chapter 9

Linn and Melanie were already in the principal's office when Phoebe arrived the next morning to pick up her monitor's badge. As she approached the door she could hear them inside, talking and laughing. The minute she walked in, they stopped.

Phoebe took a moment to glare at them stonily. Then she went up to the reception desk and requested her belt. She purposefully stood with her back to them as she arranged it. Even so, she knew that Melanie was whispering to Linn. But she resisted the urge to turn round.

She started towards the door, but Linn stepped in front of her, effectively blocking the way.

"Now, Fee," she said, "don't act like a baby." She was wearing that awful "I'm-so-mature" expression that only served to infuriate Phoebe more.

"This is the way I act round traitors," Phoebe replied coldly.

Linn gave an exaggerated sigh and shook her head sadly. "I'm not a traitor, Fee. I just wanted to help Jessica. Look, I know you wanted to be on TV. But you can't have your own way *all* the time. Right, Mel?"

Melanie's eyes darted back and forth between the two of them. "Yeah, right."

Phoebe almost laughed out loud. She couldn't

remember the last time she'd had her way with anything.

Linn put a hand on Phoebe's shoulder. "Try to be understanding."

Phoebe pulled away. "Give me a break," she snapped. It wasn't the best comeback in the world, but it was all she could manage at the moment.

Linn and Melanie exchanged looks. "Are you going to stay cross for ever?"

"I haven't decided yet," Phoebe replied. "I'll let you know." Now, *that* was a perfect exit line. Tossing her head, she left the office.

Phoebe pondered Linn's last question as she absently shoved some straying first-graders back in line. *Did* she intend to stay cross forever? It was a definite possibility. What they had done to her, depriving her of the greatest opportunity of her life, certainly justified her anger.

Still, if she did decide never to speak to them again, she'd have to make new best friends. When she went into her classroom, she paused and surveyed the room.

No one struck her as a likely candidate. And then Jessica caught her eye.

Her woeful face seemed to be sending Phoebe all kinds of messages. Phoebe was torn. On the one hand, Jessica was simply not entitled to the honour she had accepted. On the other, Phoebe couldn't be *really* nasty to someone whose mother had died. She compromised by twitching one corner of her mouth into a half-smile, but didn't speak, and then proceeded to her desk.

When Ms Lacey came in, Phoebe felt a little sick as the teacher bestowed an especially warm smile upon Jessica.

"Since Jessica is going to be representing us on television," Ms Lacey told the class, "I thought we'd spend a few moments this morning discussing the interview. I know Jessica would like to hear your ideas and opinions as to what she might contribute to the documentary."

Jessica bobbed her head eagerly and turned her desk slightly so she could see the class. She said something Phoebe could barely hear.

"Louder!" Robby yelled out.

Jessica flushed slightly, but she spoke up. "I want to do a good job."

"And you will," Ms Lacey said promptly. "Do any of you have suggestions for Jessica?"

Linn raised her hand. "I think Jessica should act very mature. Most people think sixth-graders are babies because they're still in elementary school."

Jessica nodded slowly, but she looked a little confused. "How do I do that?"

"Don't giggle," Melanie advised. "Use lots of big words and good grammar."

"Don't say *ain't*," another student added.

"I never say *ain't*," Jessica protested.

Ms Lacey seemed amused. "I don't think we need to worry about Jessica's grammar and vocabulary. She speaks very nicely."

How would she know? Phoebe wondered. Jessica hardly spoke at all. With some satisfaction, she noted

113

lines of worry beginning to form on Jessica's forehead. And there was a quaver in her voice.

"Ms Lacey, what do you think the television people are going to ask me?"

"I can't honestly say," Ms Lacey replied. "They might ask you about your career goals."

"My career goals?" Jessica echoed faintly.

Ivan's hand went up. "They'll probably ask you your opinion of elementary education."

"What should I say?" Jessica asked anxiously.

"Well, what *is* your opinion of elementary education?" Ms Lacey asked her.

"Um, it's fine, I should think."

Good grief, Phoebe thought. *Is that the best she can do? She* could think of a million things to say about elementary education. Well, it served them right if Jessica got on TV and made a fool of herself, not to mention the whole class she was supposed to be representing. That's what they got for choosing her instead of Phoebe.

"What are you going to wear?" Deirdre Callahan asked.

"I don't know," Jessica replied. Her voice was barely audible.

"I don't think that's an important question," Ms Lacey remonstrated. "Jessica always looks nice."

"But she should look especially nice," Deirdre persisted. "I mean, the whole world will be watching her."

Phoebe almost felt sorry for Jessica. She was getting very pale, and she looked like she was about to throw up. But as Ms Lacey went on to talk about the arrival of the television crew on Thursday, her heart hardened.

At lunch time, Phoebe got her tray and walked past the table where Linn, Melanie and Jessica were already sitting. Three tables away, she found one where no one was sitting.

She hated eating alone. It was like announcing to the whole world that you didn't have any friends. Out of the corner of her eye, she sneaked a peek at her usual table. Jessica was looking in her direction. Her forehead was puckered and she was biting her lower lip.

Then Phoebe saw Linn also glancing in her direction, then whispering something to Jessica. Phoebe imagined it was something like "Don't worry, she'll get over it" in her icky motherly voice.

Well, she wasn't going to get over it – not right away, at least. What was particularly infuriating was the fact that Linn hadn't even apologized. Phoebe had to show them how angry she was. And if that meant eating alone, well, she could handle it.

But there were worse things than eating alone. And with a sinking heart, Phoebe saw one of them coming towards her.

Ivan didn't ask permission to join her. He just sat down. And he didn't beat about the bush, either.

"How come you're not sitting with your friends?" he asked. His expression told Phoebe he knew perfectly well why she wasn't with her friends.

"Because I wanted to be alone," Phoebe retorted, emphasizing the word *alone*.

As usual, Ivan didn't get the message. "I don't

blame you for being angry. It was ridiculous of Ms Lacey to choose Jessica for the television programme. It's an obvious case of favouritism."

Phoebe pretended to be engrossed in her Brussels sprouts. With her fork, she peeled back the slimy green leaves as if she were searching for something.

"I knew I didn't have a chance," Ivan continued. "But she should have picked you."

Phoebe had to respond to that. "Thanks," she muttered.

"Jessica's going to do a terrible job," Ivan stated.

Privately, Phoebe agreed, but she didn't want Ivan to know that. It bothered her to be in agreement with Ivan about anything. So she just shrugged her shoulders and raised her hands in a "who knows?" gesture.

"She's stupid," Ivan said.

"She is *not*," Phoebe retorted. "She's shy, that's all." She was startled by her own outburst. What was she doing, defending Jessica?

Ivan smirked knowingly. "You're only saying that because you feel sorry for her."

Phoebe stared at him stonily. "I do *not* feel sorry for her."

Ivan leaned back in his chair. "Me neither. Besides, just because her mother died doesn't give her the right to be on television."

Her own feelings exactly. But hearing them come from Ivan's lips made them sound so – so nasty and mean. Abruptly, she stood up. "I have to go."

What a creep, she thought for the zillionth time as she returned her tray. Then she wondered: If a creep said something like that, did that make her a creep for thinking the same thing?

As she reached the cafeteria exit, she heard her name. She turned and saw Jessica hurrying towards her.

"Fee, I've got to ask you something."

She wants to know if I'm still angry, Phoebe thought. She tried to keep her face expressionless. "What?"

Jessica twisted a strand of hair that had fallen out of the tortoiseshell comb. "It's about the TV show . . . I'm really worried about it."

She didn't need to say that. Phoebe could tell. And suddenly, she felt a ray of hope. Was Jessica going to admit she couldn't handle it? Did she want Phoebe to replace her? If Jessica backed out now, Ms Lacey *had* to let Phoebe do it.

"I don't blame you for being nervous," Phoebe said. "It's going to be a pretty scary thing. All those cameras, and people asking you questions, and knowing you'll be on television where billions of people will see you." She felt reasonably sure she was describing Jessica's worst nightmare.

Jessica swallowed, and nodded. "What I was wondering . . . maybe you could help me."

"How?"

"Maybe we could get together and talk about it and practise or something . . ." her voice trailed off.

Phoebe's heart sank. She wasn't backing out. And she actually had the gall to ask Phoebe to help her!

"Sorry," she replied in a tone she usually reserved

for someone like Ivan. "I'm really busy. I don't have time."

She couldn't bring herself to look at Jessica's face. She turned quickly and fled from the cafeteria.

No one was back in the classroom yet, and Phoebe was grateful. She needed to be alone with her feelings. They were all churned up inside her, crashing and colliding and making her sick to her stomach. Her insides felt like a popcorn popper. And each kernel was a bad feeling.

In dismay, she saw Ivan come into the room. "Oh, there you are," he said. He plunked himself down on the seat across from hers. "You know, Phoebe, we ought to get together more often. I think we have a lot in common. Maybe we could be friends."

He said this as if he was bestowing some great honour on her. This time she didn't even try to be polite. That smug face of his made her even queasier.

"We could never be friends," she stated.

Ivan didn't look hurt, just curious. "Why not?"

"Because you don't know anything about being a friend!" Phoebe declared hotly. "All you do is cut people down, and tell on them, and act like you're superior to them! A friend is someone who *cares* about people. And you don't care about anyone but yourself."

Ivan's smirk was smirkier then ever. "Are you the big expert on friendship? Then how come you don't have any friends?"

Now Phoebe really thought she might throw up. She jumped up and ran out of the room. She dashed down the hall and into the sanctuary of the girls' rest room. At least Ivan couldn't follow her there.

She went into one of the cubicles and closed the door. The wave of nausea had passed, but the cubicle was still a place to hide.

When she heard the rest room door swing open, she quickly sat on the toilet and pulled up her legs so her feet wouldn't show through the opening at the bottom of the door.

Whoever you are, go away! she thought. She didn't want to see anyone. She couldn't help hearing, though. And she recognized the voices.

"Poor Jessica," Linn said. "She's an absolute wreck."

"Pretty bad," was Melanie's response.

Inside the cubicle, Phoebe scowled. Jessica was really letting this TV thing get to her.

"You can't blame Jessica for feeling awful," Linn went on. "I mean, how would you feel if someone you thought was one of your super-best friends treated you like that?"

"I can't believe Fee said she wouldn't help her," Melanie said. "That's really rotten."

"No kidding," Linn agreed. "She knows how scared Jessica is. And she doesn't even care."

Phoebe wrapped her arms around her knees and hugged herself. They didn't understand. Nobody understood. She heard the rest room door open again.

"Where were you?" Linn asked.

"I had to see Ms Lacey," Jessica's voice was low.

"We're just furious at Fee for not helping you," Melanie piped up.

Phoebe strained to hear Jessica's soft response. "Don't be mad at Fee. She didn't do anything bad."

"You just told us she wouldn't help you!" Linn exclaimed in outrage. "That's downright mean."

"She probably just wants me to stand on my own two feet," Jessica said.

"Ha!" Linn was obviously not convinced. "We had better get back to class."

Phoebe heard the door open and close, and the rest room was silent. Still huddled on the toilet seat, she could hear only the pounding of her own heart. But the echoes of her friends' words were still in her ears.

Chapter 10

When the bell rang that afternoon, Phoebe leaped from her seat. She'd almost made it to the door before she was stopped.

"Phoebe, could I see you for a minute?"

With apprehension, Phoebe looked at Ms Lacey. Had she heard about her refusal to help Jessica? Was she going to have to listen to another speech about what a terrible person she was?

As the rest of the class streamed out of the door, Phoebe made her way to the teacher's desk. She was relieved to note that Ms Lacey didn't look angry. She didn't look particularly happy, either – but at least Phoebe didn't get the feeling she was in for a lecture.

"Phoebe, it looks like Jessica won't be doing the television interview after all."

Phoebe's mouth dropped. "Why not?"

"She says she doesn't think she could do a good job." Ms Lacey spoke evenly, and she seemed to be studying Phoebe's face. "Of course, I think she's wrong about that. I'm sure it's just stage fright, and that she could overcome her fears if she tried. What do you think?"

Phoebe couldn't think anything. Her thoughts were racing too fast to catch them and put them into words. "I don't know."

"It's too bad, isn't it?" Ms Lacey mused. "Jessica's

just beginning to build up some confidence and self-esteem. This could have been a chance for her to prove something to herself. But I suppose there's nothing we can do about it, is there?"

Phoebe shook her head dumbly.

"Will you take her place?"

Phoebe wasn't sure she'd heard correctly. "You want me to be on TV?"

"Yes."

"Okay."

"Good." Ms Lacey smiled. It wasn't a big smile, but it was a smile nonetheless. "I'm sorry Jessica doesn't feel up to it, and I know you are, too. But I'm sure you'll do a fine job."

Phoebe was sure, too. She left the classroom in a daze, which lasted all through hall duty. And it was a good thing she knew the way home as well as she did, because she was in no condition to watch where she was going. Her thoughts were running wild, and images were flashing through her head like a video on fast forward.

It was going to happen. Her fantasy was coming true. The day after tomorrow, Phoebe Gray would be facing a television camera. And soon after that, she'd see herself on a TV screen. She'd be a celebrity. The whole town – no, the whole country – would know who she was. And her parents – how proud they'd be! Her sisters, too. She'd be the centre of attention, the star of the family.

It would be like the day she faced the town council and saved the banned books, only bigger and better. How great she'd felt that day, giddy with excitement, so pleased with herself. She could even remember the physical sensations, the tingles that had run through her body.

That was the way she should have been feeling now. She concentrated on the glory of it all, waiting for that special feeling to engulf her.

But it wasn't there. *It will come*, she assured herself. *It's too soon. The good news is too new, and it hasn't sunk in yet.* Tomorrow she'd feel wonderful. Or maybe the day after, when she actually faced the camera. Or maybe when she saw herself on TV. She'd be on top of the world. She'd feel it then.

But it bothered her that she wasn't feeling it right at the moment.

She had to tell somebody the news. Sharing it would bring on the good feelings. What was it her mother had once said? Something like "A pleasure shared is twice the pleasure, a pain shared is half the pain."

No one was home yet when she got there. That wasn't odd – she was usually the first one back even when she had hall duty. But she was still disappointed.

Restlessly, she wandered about the house. Then she settled in the living room and turned on the TV. But it was all soap operas and game shows, so she turned it off. She tried to read, but couldn't focus on a page. She thought about calling someone, but who? Not Linn or Melanie. And not Jessica, either.

When she heard the back door open, she went into the kitchen. Lydia was tossing her backpack on the table.

"Hi," Phoebe greeted her. She was going to follow that with "Guess what?" but something in Lydia's face made it clear her sister wasn't in the mood for exciting announcements. "What's the matter?"

Lydia unzipped her parka and plopped down heavily at the table. "Martha Jane," she said flatly. "We just had an awful fight."

For a second, Phoebe was puzzled, and then she remembered. "Oh, yeah – that Field Day thing. Was she furious because you didn't choose her?"

Lydia nodded glumly. "She said that with friends like me, she didn't need any enemies."

"That's stupid," Phoebe declared. "Like you said before, she's not right for the job."

"I know," Lydia sighed. "But I feel bad. Maybe I could have helped her with it or something." She got up, grabbed her pack, and started for the door. "I'm going to call her. Except she'll probably hang up on me."

Phoebe still felt restless. She looked in the refrigerator for something to eat and found the remains of last night's gelatine mould. She was about to pull it out when she realized she wasn't hungry at all.

She brightened when she looked out of the window and saw Daphne coming around the side of the house. At last – someone who would appreciate her news!

She didn't even give her sister time to get her coat off. "Guess what? I'm going to do the TV show after all! Jessica decided she didn't want to do it."

She'd sort of expected Daphne to clap her hands,

or hug her, or something. But for some reason, Phoebe wasn't surprised when she didn't.

"Why isn't Jessica going to do it?"

"Too shy, I guess." Phoebe sat down and drummed her fingers on the kitchen table. "You know how nervous she gets."

"Yeah." Slowly, Daphne unwrapped her scarf. "But I thought she was getting better."

"She's trying," Phoebe said. "But I guess this TV thing is too much for her to handle right now."

Daphne sighed. "Well, I'm glad you'll get to do it. But I feel sorry for Jessica. I know what it feels like to be scared of new experiences. I'll bet she's depressed about chickening out." She pulled off her coat. "I've got tons of homework. I'm going upstairs to get started."

Phoebe watched her retreating figure. Well, Daphne's reaction hadn't been what she'd hoped for. Nothing was the way she'd thought it would be. She still wasn't experiencing the thrill, the giddiness, the electric tingles that were supposed to come with good news.

She certainly wasn't feeling the way she'd felt when she planned the campaign to stop the book banners, when she stood before the Town Council and confronted them.

And then she knew why the tingles weren't there. Saving the books – that was her idea. She'd led it and organized it and made it happen. It was *her* thing.

This wasn't. This was supposed to be Jessica's. And it would have been if Phoebe had helped her. The way a friend should help a friend.

Sure, Phoebe would be good on TV. Maybe better than Jessica. And she could be the centre of attention again, and hear everyone tell her how wonderful she was.

But she wouldn't feel good about it inside. And if she didn't feel good inside, there would never be any tingles. So what was the point?

And suddenly, she knew what she was going to do, what she had to do. She got up and walked purposefully out of the kitchen and upstairs to her bedroom.

"I'm going over to Jessica's," she announced to Daphne. "Tell Mom, okay?"

And without waiting for an answer, she hurried back downstairs, grabbed her coat, and ran out of the house.

Chapter 11

She didn't have her hat, her scarf, or her mittens, but she didn't feel the cold wind. Even so, the chill was starting to penetrate by the time she reached Jessica's doorstep, and she pressed the buzzer urgently.

Jessica was obviously surprised to see her. "Fee! What are you doing here?"

Phoebe spoke through half-frozen lips. "How about letting me in and I'll tell you." Jessica obediently opened the door wider and stepped aside as Phoebe scurried in.

By the time the girls went up to Jessica's bedroom, Phoebe had thawed out. She settled herself on Jessica's bed, and got directly to the point.

"Jess, why did you tell Ms Lacey you couldn't do the TV show?"

Jessica suddenly seemed intent on straightening up her room. She took a sweater off the bed, and with her back to Phoebe, began folding it precisely.

"C'mon, Jess," Phoebe pressed.

Jessica continued to work on the sweater, but she spoke. "I guess I just freaked out. I was afraid those TV people might ask me questions I couldn't answer."

"Like what?"

"I don't know." She carried the sweater to her dresser, opened a drawer, and carefully laid it inside.

"Ms Lacey asked me to take your place."

Jessica started rearranging some china figurines on top of her dresser. "That's nice. I know you wanted to do it. And you'll be better at it than I would be."

True, Phoebe thought wistfully. But she didn't say it. "That doesn't matter. Ms Lacey picked *you*. That means she thinks you'd be the best person."

"Maybe she's wrong," Jessica suggested.

"Jessica!" Phoebe exclaimed. "She's a teacher!"

Jessica finally left the dresser and sat down on the bed. "You think I should do it?"

Phoebe nodded. Jessica studied her bitten finger-nails, as if she was searching for something to chew on.

"You know you can do it," Phoebe stated. "You're getting braver all the time. Even Ms Lacey noticed how much you've changed. Ever since your mother died – "

She stopped herself abruptly, but it was too late. Jessica promptly burst into tears.

Oddly enough, though, her crying didn't terrify Phoebe the way she thought it would. She took Jessica's hand, squeezed it, and just let her cry.

"I miss her," Jessica wept.

"I know," Phoebe said softly. With her free hand, she reached for the box of tissues on the nightstand. For the next few moments, Jessica sobbed quietly. Still holding her hand, Phoebe remembered again what her mother had said about a pleasure shared being twice the pleasure and a pain shared half the pain. She tried to share Jessica's pain. It wasn't a very difficult thing to do. And then she was crying, too.

Jessica took a tissue and wiped her eyes. Phoebe took another and blew her nose.

"My mother," Jessica said in a halting voice, "she told me there was a brave person inside me who was trying to get out. And she said I shouldn't be afraid of her."

"She was right," Phoebe said. "You know, when you volunteered to get the light bulb at school, that was the brave part of you coming out."

Jessica nodded. "And I was so scared. But afterwards, I felt great."

"That's how you'll feel if you do the TV show."

Jessica wiped her eyes again. "Yeah. I guess so."

"And think how proud your mother would be."

"Mmmm." Jessica's brow furrowed. "But what if they ask me questions I can't answer? Like this morning, in class. I didn't know what to say."

"That's just because you weren't thinking and you weren't prepared," Phoebe said. "You panicked."

"What if I panic on TV?"

"You won't," Phoebe said positively. "Because you'll be prepared. I'll help you."

"You will?" Jessica's eyes, still wet from the tears, were shining.

"I'll call home and tell them I'm spending the night here, okay?"

"That would be great!" As Phoebe got up and headed out to the hall, Jessica added, "Oh Fee, I'm so lucky to have a friend like you!"

Phoebe felt a little pang. She really hadn't been much of a friend these past few days. But she was going to make up for it now. Even if it took all night.

✳ ✳ ✳

Phoebe didn't dare look at the clock on Jessica's nightstand. It had to be after midnight. Dinner had been a long time ago, and the silence in the house told her Mr Duncan had gone to bed.

Jessica was flat on her back. "I feel like I'm going to fall asleep right this minute."

Phoebe stifled a yawn. "Okay, let's just try once more. Now, I'm the interviewer." She deepened her voice to a low growl. "Miss Duncan, what has been your most difficult experience in elementary school?"

Jessica wrinkled her nose. "Do you really think they're going to call me 'Miss Duncan'?"

Phoebe considered this. "Probably not," she admitted. Adults never had that much respect for kids, even if they were on television. "Okay, *Jessica*. What's the hardest thing about elementary school?"

Jessica closed her eyes briefly, then opened them. "Ropes."

"What?"

"Climbing the ropes in phys ed. I can only get halfway up."

"And do you feel ropes are vital for your career goals?" Phoebe-the-Interviewer asked.

"Absolutely," Jessica replied. "I mean, what if I end up working on the top floor of a high rise and the elevator breaks down?"

"Have you never heard of stairs?" Phoebe inquired.

Jessica sat up. "Gee, they haven't taught us about stairs yet. Maybe we get that in junior high."

It wasn't all that funny, but Phoebe couldn't help giggling. That got Jessica started too, although her combination of giggles and yawns made it sound like she was gasping. Phoebe cracked up. She snatched a pillow and pounded Jessica on the head. Jessica grabbed the other pillow and returned fire.

The battle didn't last too long.

"Girls!" came a voice from across the hall. "Go to sleep!"

"Okay, Dad!" Jessica called back.

Phoebe forced herself up off Jessica's bed, practically tripping on the too-long pajamas she'd borrowed. She climbed into the other bed.

Jessica got under the covers and turned off the light. "Ms Lacey is going to be surprised tomorrow when I tell her I changed my mind. What do you think she'll say?"

"I don't know," Phoebe replied faintly. "But she'll be glad."

"I'm still a little nervous. But I think I'm going to be okay."

"Uh-uh," Phoebe said. "Better than okay."

"I just wish my mother could see me on TV," Jessica whispered.

Phoebe rolled over and faced her. "She's watching you from heaven, remember?"

"Yeah. Fee?"

"What?"

"Do you think there are TVs in heaven?"

"Absolutely," Phoebe mumbled. "Probably giant-screen ones. With stereo. And remote control."

"And cable," Jessica murmured. "You think they've got cable?"

"Mmmm . . . zillions of channels." The image of a video heaven made Phoebe want to start giggling again. Only she didn't have the energy for anything more than falling asleep.

Chapter 12

"Ms Lacey says they'll probably show our whole class on TV," Phoebe told her mother on the way to school on Thursday morning. "But Jessica will probably be the only one who gets to talk."

"I'm so pleased she's doing this," Mrs Gray remarked. "It's a real achievement for her."

Phoebe agreed, but in all fairness, she deserved a tiny bit of credit. "I helped her a lot, you know."

"You certainly did," her mother said. "And it was very unselfish of you to help her when you wanted the job yourself."

Phoebe gazed at her in astonishment. "How did you know that? Did Daphne tell you?"

"Just an educated guess, Fee. I know my daughters." She paused at a stop sign, and looked at Phoebe sympathetically. "It couldn't have been easy for you. I wish you'd talked to me about it. I might have been able to help."

"Sorry, Mom. But I knew what you would say. You'd tell me Jessica deserved some happiness, and that I shouldn't be jealous."

Mrs Gray smiled. "You're probably right. I guess you know your mother." She paused. "Were you jealous?"

"A little," Phoebe admitted. Then she grinned. "A lot. But I guess it's better for Jessica to do it. I mean,

I would have been good. But Jessica needs to do something like this."

Her mother looked enormously pleased to hear this. "That's a very mature attitude, Fee. I'm proud of you. Very proud. And I know your father will be, too."

"Really? Even more proud than if I'd been on TV?"

"Absolutely."

Phoebe considered this. Making sacrifices obviously had some benefits. She'd definitely scored some points with this one.

There was a big van parked in front of the school, with the letters of a television station prominently displayed on its side. Phoebe shivered. This was going to be exciting, even if all she got to do was watch. She endured an unusually fervent hug from her mother before tearing out of the car and running into the building.

Ms Lacey had asked everyone to get there early, so the classroom was just about full, and much noisier than usual. Everyone was dressed better than usual, too. Linn looked positively glamorous in a navy blue suit, and Melanie had a velvet hairband in her curls. When they spotted Phoebe, they waved.

Phoebe headed towards them. Thank goodness they were all friends again. Yesterday, Jessica had told them how Phoebe had helped her. And no one was angry with her any more.

"You look great," Phoebe told her. "You too, Mel." She didn't tell Melanie that there was a stain on her collar that looked like egg yolk.

134

"Oodle oodle," Melanie squealed, and Linn didn't even glare at her for using Doodlebug language. Phoebe could tell she was just as excited as everyone else.

"Are you sure I look okay?" Linn asked, adjusting her suit jacket. "I heard that the camera adds ten pounds to a person. So I thought I'd better wear something dark and slimming."

"Ten pounds?" Phoebe looked down at her own jumper. She had a feeling red wasn't very slimming.

"Here comes the star of the show!" Melanie cried out.

Jessica approached them with a smile that seemed frozen on her face. "Do I look all right?"

Phoebe checked out her bright green sweater and skirt, and nodded approvingly. "You look terrific. And you can use the extra ten pounds."

"Huh?"

Just then the classroom door opened. A woman carrying a clipboard strode in and went directly to Ms Lacey. "Are you the teacher?"

"Yes, I'm Ms Lacey."

"I'm the director, Jane Wilson." They shook hands, and then the woman turned to the open door. "Okay, guys, this is the right room."

Phoebe gaped at the parade that marched into the room. First came a fat man with a big video camera. He was followed by a woman carrying headphones and some other stuff Phoebe couldn't identify. Then there was a man with something that looked like a gigantic lamp.

"Just go ahead with your usual routine while we set up," the director told Ms Lacey. "Ignore us."

Ms Lacey stared at her in disbelief, but clapped her hands and told the class to settle down. Of course, nobody did.

"Are you feeling okay?" Phoebe asked Jessica quietly. She couldn't tell if it was the sweater that was making Jessica's face look a little green, or something else.

"I think so," Jessica said carefully. Her eyes were fixed on all the strangers. Phoebe watched her anxiously. Then she had an inspiration.

"Remember what your mother said. Pretend they're all in their underwear."

Jessica looked like she was concentrating. Then her mouth twitched. "Even the one with the big stomach?"

Phoebe looked at the cameraman. "Especially the one with the big stomach."

"Class!" Ms Lacey called out. "Please take your seats and be quiet. The television people want to begin."

Phoebe gave Jessica a *V* for *victory* sign and headed towards her seat. On the way, she started to pass Ivan, and then she paused. She felt sorry for him. He didn't have the slightest idea what friendship was all about. And unless he changed his ways, he'd never know how good it felt to be happy for someone else.

She wanted to say something to him. But all she could think of were some lines she'd seen on a greeting card. "You know, Ivan, if you really want a friend, you have to *be* a friend." Okay, maybe that wasn't very original or brilliant, but it was true.

Ivan looked at her blankly, as if she were speaking a foreign language. Phoebe sighed and moved on to her seat. Poor Ivan. Maybe, someday, he'd find out what he was missing.

Ms Lacey gave the class a once-over, straightening a few desks and removing an oversize pink and yellow bow tie from Robby. Then Jane Wilson took over.

"I want you all to behave perfectly naturally and normally," she told the class.

Fat chance, Phoebe thought. She sat up straight and smiled in a way she would never normally smile in school. Maybe when the camera shot the class, someone would notice her happy face and give her a close-up.

The big light went on, and the man with the camera began to shoot the room, moving the camera from one side to the other. With the bright light in her eyes, Phoebe couldn't tell if the camera was pointed in her direction. It was all over in a few minutes, anyway.

Then Jane Wilson clipped something on the neck of Jessica's sweater. "This is a microphone. Just pretend it's not there."

Phoebe could only see the back of Jessica's head bob. She wondered what colour her face was. *Do well, Jess*, she thought fiercely. She held her breath as Jane Wilson spoke.

"Jessica, this is your last year in elementary school. How do you feel about that?"

The room was deadly silent. And then Jessica's voice could be heard – not loud, but clear.

"It's a little sad, I guess. It's like something nice is ending. But something new will be starting. Only we don't know what it will be like in junior high, so it's a little scary."

"Do you think your elementary education had prepared you for junior high?"

"I don't know," Jessica replied. "I mean, I've never been to junior high so how do I know if I'm prepared for it?"

Slowly, silently, Phoebe let out her breath. Jessica was going to do just fine. And Phoebe started to feel a little tingly. Okay, maybe they weren't the thrilling, electric tingles she'd had when she saved the banned books. But they were nice tingles, nonetheless. They told her she was feeling happy for Jessica.

Jane Wilson asked more questions, and Jessica answered them. As her fears for Jessica wore off, Phoebe began fantasizing about the way she would have answered the questions. She couldn't help it. It was all very nice and noble to make sacrifices, but she'd still rather be a star. And she could have been a star, if she hadn't decided to help Jessica. But then she would have had to live with those bad feelings. It probably wasn't worth it.

"What do you like best about school, Jessica?" Jane Wilson asked.

Say maths, Phoebe thought. That would impress them.

But Jessica didn't say that. "Being with my friends." She turned, and the cameraman turned to follow her. She pointed a finger at Phoebe. "That's one of my best friends right there. Phoebe Gray."

Phoebe was stunned. And when she heard Jane Wilson tell the cameraman to get a shot of her, she froze. When the camera focused on her, she wasn't even sure if she was smiling or not.

Then the camera moved away. Jane Wilson was talking to Jessica again. And Phoebe sank back in her seat.

So she was going to be on TV after all. Only for a second, though. Not long enough to make her a star.

Well, maybe she wouldn't be a star, but an awful lot of people would know she was somebody's friend. And she decided she wouldn't mind becoming famous for that.

Also in
Lions Tracks

To order direct from the publisher, just tick the titles you want and fill in the order form on the last page.

My Darling, My Hamburger

Paul Zindel

This is the story of two girls. Maggie is the plain, shy dark one who despairs of ever making herself attractive enough to have a boyfriend. Blonde Liz is pretty enough to get herself plenty of dates but doesn't know how to handle them. From her teacher the only advice she's given on how to stop a guy on the make is to suggest going for a hamburger; from her stepfather come accusations of behaving like a little tramp by staying out late – which is what finally drives her bitterly into giving her boyfriend what he wants. The consequences are tragic for herself, the boy and Maggie.

Against the background of the American high school scene, Paul Zindel has written a novel which is funny, sad, moving and grimly ironic in its acceptance of the complete lack of communication between many teenagers and their parents.

'He is the most interesting and adventurous writer of the contemporary novel for teenagers at work on either side of the Atlantic. In his hands the teenage book comes of age.' *Times Educational Supplement*

The Pigman, I Never Loved Your Mind, and *Pardon Me, You're Stepping on My Eyeball!* are also in Lions Tracks.

LIONS · TRACKS

It's My Life

Robert Leeson

"You're playing hard to get," Sharon had said as Jan walked off, away from school and from Peter Carey's invitation to the college disco on Friday night. Was she? Jan didn't really know. She wanted time to think things out, ask Mum what she thought.

But when Mum doesn't come home, Jan finds her own problems taking second place, as she is expected to cope with running the house for her father and younger brother Kevin, as well as studying for exams and trying to sort out her feelings towards Peter. Slowly she realises what sort of life her mother led, the loneliness and the pressures she faced, and with this realisation comes Jan's firm resolve that despite the expectations of family, neighbours and friends, she will decide things for herself; after all, "It's my life."

Tex

S. E. Hinton

Tex, at fifteen, is easygoing, likes everyone and every-thing. Life is just fine until he comes home from school one day to find his horse Negrito has been sold by his older brother Mason to pay the mounting household bills. From then on things get uglier. Tex begins to resent his father's lengthy, unexplained absences, but Mason, high school sports star, is hungry for success, eager for the university scholarship that will be his passport out of their hick town. When 'Pop' returns, relaxed and absent-minded as ever, he is unconcerned about the increasing amount of trouble Tex is in at school. But Mason seems determined to force matters to a head, and for Tex the truths revealed are almost as devastating physically as they are emotionally.

'S. E. Hinton is at her talented best in *Tex*. A justly renowned pioneer of the hot novel, her sentences surge from the page.' *The Guardian*

The Outsiders, *That Was Then, This is Now* and *Rumble Fish* by S. E. Hinton are also available in Lions Tracks.

oks are available at your local
 r newsagent, or can be
 the publishers.

 ct from the publishers just
 ...titles you want and fill in the form
below:

Name _____

Address _____

_____

Send to: Collins Children's Cash Sales
         PO Box 11
         Falmouth
         Cornwall
         TR10 9EN

Please enclose a cheque or postal order or debit my Visa/
Access –

    Credit card no:

    Expiry date:

    Signature:

– to the value of the cover price plus:

UK: 60p for the first book, 25p for the second book, plus
15p per copy for each additional book ordered to a
maximum charge of £1.90.

BFPO: 60p for the first book, 25p for the second book, plus
15p per copy for the next 7 books, thereafter 9p per book.

Overseas and Eire: £1.25 for the first book, 75p for the
second book. Thereafter 28p per book.

Lions reserve the right to show new retail prices on covers which may differ from
those previously advertised in the text or elsewhere.

Lions Tracks